D0887001

CITY BOYS

Stories by

DAVID LEWIS STEIN

"The Avenue" (page 5) is an excerpt from a forthcoming novel entitled *Taking Power*. "The Night of the Little Brown Men" (page 97) is reprinted from *Saturday Night* and *New Canadian Writing 1968* (Clarke, Irwin), "The Demonstration, 1" (page 122) from *Scratch One Dreamer* (McClelland & Stewart), "The Demonstration, 2" (page 131) from *Living the Revolution: The Yippies in Chicago* (Bobbs-Merrill), "The Demonstration, 3" (page 145) from *My Sexual and Other Revolutions* (New Press). "Back Where I Can Be Me" (page 113) first appeared in *Impulse*, "Fresh Disasters" (page 148) in *Saturday Night*. "Marvin, Marvin" (page 37) and "In There" (page 172) are published here for the first time.

ISBN 0 88750 274 1 (hardcover)
ISBN 0 88750 276 8 (softcover)

Editor: David Helwig. Designer: Michael Macklem

Printed in Canada

PUBLISHED IN CANADA BY OBERON PRESS

For Alison, who was there too

The Avenue

Max Himmelfarb parks the Cadillac in front of a dry-cleaning plant. The barren little shopping plaza stirs memories. Max had to push the Englanders into gambling on even these scraggly little blocks of stores. If it hadn't been for Max, they'd have gone on building little shitbox bungalows forever. Probably they would have gone broke in the great recession of the Diefenbaker years. But Max pushed the Englanders into commercial and then into office buildings and finally into the great sprawling shopping plazas, Eastern Market and Ontario Square. Those joints made everybody rich, even the lawyers. Who else but Max Himmelfarb had the vision to know what incredible gold mines would grow out of these little asphalt parking-lots, each with its own row of shitbox stores? And how did the Englanders show their appreciation after all these years? They threw him out of the company.

The apartment above the constant whine of the dry-cleaning plant is dark and stale; Nora Besser waits at the top of the stairs. The years have not been kind. The famous red hair is black now with dye and stiff with age.

"Another country heard from," Nora says. She thrusts out her white cheek for Max to kiss.

"What do you want, Max?"

"I just heard about Jake."

Nora nods her head in assent but it is more like a bow and she rises as though she is recovering from a blow. She leads Max into the bedroom. A wheelchair rests against the wall. The old brass double bed, the only thing Nora took from the apartment on Berryman Avenue, has been replaced by a hospital cot. And even this looks too big for Jake. He lies gasping even in his sleep, his useless legs tangled in the stiff, white hospital sheets. Who would ever believe Jake Besser could be so thin? How can anybody look so frail and still live?

"You get my cheques?" Max says.

"Yes—they're a big help, Max. They wanted to send Jake to a nursing home but I went out and looked at a couple of those places and I said, 'No, Jake'll die in here. You send him home to me and I'll look after him.'"

Max settles down in an easy chair and lights up a cigar while he waits for Jake to wake up. He is reassured to see there is still something left of the old Jake. The hands lying open on the sheets are big and solid as ever.

Remember the time they were sitting in Jake's old DeSoto convertible on Queen Street and Bartleman came up and told them to move the car? Max would have done it because who needs that kind of trouble with the cops? But Jake told him very quietly to leave them alone. Bartleman was a big man and he wasn't afraid of anyone. He kept bothering Jake. Finally Jake stepped out of the car and knocked him out. With one punch he knocked the cop cold. There was never another like Jake Besser.

"Where you been, Max?" Nora says.

"I don't know."

This is not what Max intended to say. He wanted only to answer Nora's bitterness, to explain why he has just come to visit now even though Jake had the stroke five months ago. He wanted only to make his excuses to Nora but something else came out.

I don't know where I have been. I was here and I was young. And now I am old and I am here again. And I don't know what happened to all that time in between.

Jake stirs on the bed. The panting becomes louder, more desperate, as though something inside his chest were breaking. Jake reaches for the glasses on the ashtray. After a long time he raises himself on one elbow, the milky eyes focus on Max.

"You look good," Jake says. "You must be making lots of money."

"But he don't forget his friends," Nora says. "You know somethin' Max? If it wasn't for your cheques coming in every month, we couldn't live."

"I read about you in the papers," Jake says. "You're a big shot now, eh? You did all right for yourself."

Max feels at ease with Jake's bitterness, as though someone had applied a cold compress to his own soul. So it would have made no difference after all if he had stayed in the rackets. No matter which road he'd chosen, he would have wound up in the same place. All roads lead in the end to defeat. If there were some young man who trusted him enough to ask advice, Max would have said this was the final lesson of life. You always lose.

"If you'd stuck with me, we coulda took over this town," Jake says. "We coulda been kings. But you was too nervous. You was always a very nervous kid, you know that?"

"I'll tell you something, Jake. It wasn't no bed of roses for me either. Twenty-five years I worked for the Englanders, and you know what they did? They pushed me out. They stuck a knife in me, Jake."

"You can't trust no-one," Jake says. "Didn't I always tell you that?"

"You did and you were right, Jake. They didn't even thank me when they kicked me out."

Jake smiles, very pleased. Max takes a couple of Tueros cigars from his jacket pocket. Jake Besser, he knows, would be amused if Max told him they cost a dollar each. When Jake was trying to impress him in the old days with how important a man was, Jake always said he smoked dollar cigars. Max pulls the cigars from their tin-foil tubes and gives one to Jake. Nora starts to fuss about it, then seeing the look in Jake's eyes, she comes to the bed and sits behind Jake and holds him up propped against her. Max lights the cigar for him, and settles back in his own chair.

"What the hell was wrong with Johnny Bartleman?" Max says.

"Bartleman? He was my partner," Jake says.

"You never told me that!"

"There's a whole lot of things I never told you," Jake says. He laughs again and rests against Nora's shoulder. It's so long since he has tasted a good cigar. If the doctors knew, they'd have a fit. But to Nora, the two men sitting together and the heavy, musty smell of their cigars filling up the room brings back memories of the apartment over Steadman's and the characters on Berryman Avenue. Where are they all today? Nora wonders. Are they all as bad off as Jake? Did any of them do all right in life? Nora shifts her weight so she can hold Jake up more comfortably.

"You remember Steadman, the guy who owned the restaurant?" Jake says.

"Sure. Every time I come in the door, he starts cutting me a corned-beef sandwich. I couldn't order anything else from him. By the time I sit down at the counter he's already got a corned-beef sandwich in front of me."

"Steadman was my partner too," Jake says.

"No!" Max says. "I always thought the old man was legit."

"Them days," Jake says. "Them days..."

For a young man in the years after World War II, Berryman Avenue was a day-long, night-long carnival. Everybody was there. Everything was happening. Max Himmelfarb could come downstairs from his apartment at any time and there was always something to do, a crap game, a klabbiash game, shooting pool, hunting for gash, kibitzing with friends, maybe getting into a little trouble running with the chicken thieves; or maybe just somebody to talk to, the old-timers cursing the world in their bitter, savoury Yiddish, or the young kids, friends of Max's brothers, hanging around in front of Steadman's restaurant, lounging against the hoods of the cars, bragging, boasting, wrestling on the street, cocky as hell. They always had a place for Max Himmelfarb. They listened to what he had to say. Max Himmelfarb was nineteen years old and he was already known on the street as a man who was going to make something of himself.

Max was in love with two people. Max felt filled to the brim with love. First, there was Jake Besser who lived over Steadman's. Jake was a bootlegger and a bookmaker. Max was his runner. He travelled the city every night in Jake's car, collecting from the losers and paying off the winners. Sometimes in the afternoons he sat for hours in Jake Besser's apartment while Jake worked the street and called in bets from the phone booth at Steadman's.

Jake Besser was more than a boss. Jake was a friend. Max had left home. There was no money at home, only shouting and screaming. Jake was his real family. Jake had no children of his own and probably he had never wanted any. Who could picture Jake Besser with his wide-brimmed Sammy Taft fedora and his thick black overcoat pushing a baby carriage? Jake never said anything corny, like calling Max a pal or a sidekick. Max was part of the bookmaking side of Jake's operation and every Monday afternoon, after he had had his onions and eggs in Steadman's and figured out the week's gains and losses in a little black notebook, Jake paid him $50. If Max wanted to hang around and get involved in other things, that was Max's own business.

One of the reasons Max loved Jake was that Jake never told him what to do or think. In Jake Besser's company, Max always felt like a grown man. His life was his own.

Sometimes, if the week had been especially good, Jake would throw in an extra $10 bill. "Here, get yourself an ice-cream cone on the way home," Jake always said. And then he laughed that wonderful, bitter snarling laugh that Max could never quite emulate. Only a man who had travelled with the Purple Mob in Detroit and been in Chicago and New York and done time — Jake had been seven years in Kingston—could laugh at the world the way Jake Besser laughed.

When he was not working out with weights at the Y or

shooting pool in the New Yorker Billiard Academy with pals from Club Morgan, Max was hanging around Jake Besser. He took the car to the liquor store to get the weekend's supply of rye and scotch. He went shopping with Nora, Jake Besser's beautiful wife, and carried home the bags of groceries and kosher chickens for her. On slow afternoons, when there wasn't a bet to be had on Berryman, Max even took the Bessers' toy poodle over to Queen's Park for a romp and a kibitz.

There were people who believed that Max Himmelfarb was heading for trouble. The foot patrolmen who plodded up and down Berryman Avenue all said that over their morning coffee at the counter at Steadman's. The detectives and inspectors who drank tumblers of straight whisky at Jake's kitchen table all weekend said it too. When the Sunday morning sunlight finally blasted them loose, they would put on their overcoats getting ready to finally go home and fix their mean eyes on the swarthy, smiling Jewboy sitting beside Nora Besser at the piano and singing songs with her. How could he still look as fresh as a daisy? "That punk's looking for trouble," Johnny Bartleman, the Sergeant of Detectives, always said. "That little punk don't know what he's getting into."

Max knew what the police thought of him but he didn't worry about it very much. He had other things on his mind. He was in love with Shelley Englander and he was sure that fortune was waiting just ahead of him. He had known for years that he was a little different and, to be honest, a little better than other people. It wasn't only the boys hanging out on Berryman Avenue who knew that Max Himmelfarb was going to be a success some day. Max knew it too. That was one of the reasons Shelley Englander loved him in return. Max was sure beyond the slightest quavering of doubt that when the time was ripe, success would simply happen to him. Until then, he could relax and love Shelley and enjoy his life.

Shelley Englander's hair was as black as coal and as strong as wire. Her eyes, when she was not laughing, were dark too. When she was being serious, her eyes wrinkled up with hurt. She looked then like a wise old woman. But people who only saw Shelley and did not know her some-how always thought of her as fair and light. Shelley had a wisecrack for everything. Half the time she didn't even understand the sexy double meanings of the things she said. But that never mattered. Shelley laughed along with everyone else. Everyone loved her. Only with Max Him-melfarb did she let her serious side show. Only with Max did she sometimes let the tears come while she talked about her father and the terrible hate-filled house that she lived in.

Mostly she went with Max to dances at the Y or to parties in the Club Morgan clubrooms or to parties at her girl friends' houses. The boys in Club Morgan had a bad reputation but Shelley was never afraid to be with Max. His hands were so gentle and soft on her skin. He always smelled so good to her, like olive oil and spices. Shelley always relied on Max never to let her get carried away by her own strong feelings and never to press too hard him-self. She knew she had entered the most dangerous period of a woman's life. She trusted Max to see her through. She loved him.

Max took her once to Jake's on a Saturday night and a crap game got going. Shelley loved it. She was jumping up and down beside Jake yelling "Come on! Come on! Come on! Come on!" Everyone was laughing. They seemed so old to Shelley and Max, these bookies, police detectives, cab drivers, and street hustlers; so old and thick with scars. But they were grinning like little children when they watched Shelley cheering Jake on. Max glowed with pride. The only other woman who had ever been in Jake's was Jake's own wife, Nora. Now this beautiful young girl with the enormous breasts was there, lighting up the place, and she belonged to him. Other men could enjoy her laughter and other men could desire her but she was going to walk out of there with Max. Jake won $300 that night. Nora opened a bottle of fine old French brandy she had been saving and poured everyone a free drink. She played the piano and just for the hell of it, just to give the old men a thrill, Max and Shelley did some jitterbugging.

Shelley never told Max what happened to her after he brought her home that night from Jake's. They sat in Jake's car in front of her house for a long time and when Max finally drove away and Shelley went in, the sky was already turning pearly grey. Her younger brothers, Karl and Fred, were waiting nervously in the flowered living-room. Shelley's lipstick was smeared and the tail of her blouse hung out. At the top of the stairs, her mother slapped her face.

Her mother called her a whore in Yiddish and stood in the dark, oak hallway slapping Shelley's face until Shelley's head was ringing.

But Shelley didn't cry out and she didn't turn away. Downstairs, her brother Fred winced with the sound of each blow and her brother Karl sat awestruck and dumb, staring up at a scene he could not see for the darkness. The sound of the slapping slowed down. Mrs. Englander's fury drained away. Finally she stopped and stared at her daughter, looking anxiously for some sign of pain or contrition. But Shelley only stepped past her without a word and went into her own bedroom and closed the door behind her.

The next day the old man, Isidore Englander himself, came up Berryman Avenue like a hungry trout. He found Max at the back table in the New Yorker Billiard Academy.

All the games stopped. All the players turned to gape at this vision from the past with his iron face and death-black suit.

Only Max Himmelfarb did not stop. He was shooting pool with his best boyfriend from Club Morgan and he took his turn and cleaned the table off. Twelve balls in a row he sank, the best run anyone could ever remember seeing Max make. Clickety-click the balls went and the other players in the New Yorker began to relax and smirk. Only when he had won the game and collected $12 in side bets and put his cue back in the rack, did Max acknowledge the father of the girl he was in love with. Mr. Englander's face was red with anger but he was an old man and he was used to waiting for the things he wanted. He always got them in the end.

"Hello, Mr. Englander," Max said. "You looking for me?"

The old man had a deal to offer. He took Max to the offices of the Premier Paint and Plastering Company across the street from the Minsker Shule and offered him a job. He was impressed by Max, he said. Everybody told him what a smart boy Max Himmelfarb was and wasn't it a shame he was getting in so deep with the racketeers.

Well, Englander needed a young man who was smart and willing to work hard. The company was ready to expand. His own two sons were useless. Nice boys, mind you, and his own flesh and blood, but neither one of them had any head for business. One was going to be a doctor and the other was in university and still didn't know what he wanted to do. Max would have to start off with the plasterers and painters to learn the business but once he had and could show the old man that he knew what he was talking about, then Mr. Englander said he was going to take him into the office. He didn't exactly say he was offering him a partnership but it was pretty clear to Max that was what the old man had in mind. He never once mentioned Shelley.

Max wasn't even tempted. Mr. Englander was too much like the men his father despised so passionately. Max's father had learned the trade of making vests and he was very good at it. He had worked all through the depression for Eaton's and managed to support his family quite comfortably while other men who had come from Poland at the same time were on relief. But then the war came and vests were considered a waste of cloth essential to the war effort. Max's father was reduced to operating a big steam press for jackets and trousers. The heat and the moist air gave him chronic bronchitis but still he refused to change what he knew. Day after day, Max's father pulled down the big handle and stood alone surrounded by curls of biting steam. And when anyone was brash enough to talk to him, he cursed Max's mother. If only she had let him take the money out of the bank and go into business when he wanted to, he would be a rich man. Other men who had gone into making and selling clothes during the war were swelling into millionaires now that the war was over and people had money again. Max's father envied and hated those men and he could talk of nothing else. Max often thought of the cleaning plant where his father worked as a kind of miniature hell, filled with white, hissing fire and screaming devils.

Isidore Englander had been only a housepainter before the war. But when the war ended, and people were building new places to live or trying to fix up old ones, suddenly housepainters and handymen were in great demand. Mr. Englander hired two friends to work for him. Now he had seven painters and four plasterers. And there was more work than they could handle. He was offering Max an opportunity that other young men would leap at.

But Max could only shake his head. If this old man had not been Shelley's father, Max would have said something harsh and irretrievable to him. Did this old man really believe Max would sell himself so cheaply?

"Don't make up your mind so quick," the old man Englander said. "My Rochelle tells me how intelligent you are. So when a man is thinking of getting married and raising a family, he needs to know where his next dollar is coming from."

"Thanks," Max said. "But I've got other plans."

Max was absolutely sure that working for his father-in-law in the Premier Paint Company was not the kind of success fate was saving up for him.

Still, he did need money. Old man Englander had been right about that much, anyway. For a long afternoon, Max lay with his hands behind his head staring up at the office-green ceiling of his apartment and seeing only his own life. Max liked to tell people he was actually living alone in his own apartment but in fact, it was more like a broom closet. Club Morgan had rented three rooms above the Royal Bank in the old Cawthra Building on Berryman Avenue. They had once been offices and there was a fourth, adjoining room that had once been used for storing files. It had no windows. Max paid an extra $5 a month in dues to the club for the use of this room. There was space in it only for an iron cot and beside the cot, leaving only a narrow alleyway, a dresser Max had brought from home and a wardrobe he had bought from a second-hand store so he would have a place to hang up his strides. After talking to Englander, it came to Max with a sickening jolt that these three pieces of furniture were the only things in the world he owned.

Time, he saw with painful clarity now, as though the

foolish mist of his other life had suddenly been blown away, time was passing him by. The boys from Club Morgan lived on three blocks that flowed into Berryman Avenue like tributary streams. They had been together all through public school, and in grade eight they had decided to form a club because who could tell? High school might separate them and drive them apart. But now high school was over. The good times would end soon. The boys had all been living on the momentum of high school. Max had always thought of Sir Edward Langleigh Collegiate Institute as a stuffy, boring place. He had left at the end of grade twelve, as soon as he could legally get away. But looking back, the teachers he had thought he hated were now only characters to laugh about. So many good stories the boys could tell when they got together. So many good times they had had, the basketball team, the parties and dances, the kibitzes, the long Saturday nights just hanging out together walking up and down Berryman Avenue, looking for something to happen. In those days something always did. Four years of good times, but now they were all gone and they would never come again. Max laughed bitterly to himself in the afternoon loneliness of his little apartment. Chances were if he stayed there, he would be alone all night too. Only a year ago, less than that, there had been something going on every night at Club Morgan. Now the boys came only on the weekends and if they hadn't organized a party, all they wanted to do was sit around and play cards.

Six of the boys had gone to university and they talked about things that Max didn't even understand. The others were all working in factories or selling in stores but nobody expected them to stay working men forever. It was only a matter of time, probably a very short time, until they got a little money together and went into business on their own.

Already, two of the boys had borrowed money from an uncle and opened a cut-rate men's-wear store out in the Junction. The boys in Club Morgan had already lived so hard and done so much in their lives that even though they were still young men, they had built up a momentum that would carry them far beyond Berryman Avenue. Everyone knew the boys in Club Morgan were something special.

Only Max seemed to be going nowhere. It did not seem possible to Max that he could have gone past the turning point in his life without even knowing it. Yet maybe it was true. His love for Jake Besser might well have doomed him before he even got started. Where was he to get the money to buy Shelley out of the bitter clasp of the Englander family? Money was the only thing the Englanders understood.

Jake was sympathetic. He didn't have much cash himself but he took a diamond ring out of a teapot in the kitchen and offered it to Max. They were sitting in Jake's kitchen early the next morning and Jake was making them coffee. Nora was still asleep and Jake had come to the door to let Max in wearing only his boxer shorts stamped with a design of stripes and polka dots as elaborate as a necktie and his white undershirt. Watching him, Max was sure that he had made the right choice after all. Even at this ungodly hour, even padding around in his underwear, Jake looked like New York. Jake Besser conducted his life with an easiness and grace that the Englanders, if they all lived to be a thousand and all became millionaires, could never understand or match.

"Give me ten bucks for that," Jake said, dropping the ring on the table in front of Max. "You ought to be able to get 100, maybe 200, for that out on the street. Guy out of Chicago left it here last night. He didn't have no cash either. Pretty, ain't it?"

The ring became a terrible burden for Max. Common sense told him to sell it and put the money in the bank. Every bit of cash he accumulated was another step toward claiming Shelley. Yet the ring was so beautiful. Time after time in the days that followed he took the ring out of his pocket and studied it. It was thick and it seemed to be made of very old gold, almost the colour of brass. It rose to a crown as delicate as lace. From the crown, little hooks rose to hold the diamond. Under the light the diamond glinted with such radiance that it was hard to see its real shape or even to tell how large it was. He asked Jake once if the guy out of Chicago had ever said how he happened to have such a ring. Jake laughed. "His company makes them," Jake said. "US Steal."

One of the jewellers Max tried to sell the ring to told him the diamond was heavier than two carats and the ring was over a hundred years old. He offered Max $350 for it. Max turned him down. After all, if it was worth 350 to that little schmock, it was probably worth twice that to somebody else. His only problem was to find the right buyer. Max looked for three weeks. Every time someone made him a good offer, he raised the price. Finally, he gave the ring to Shelley.

All his life he remembered the first time she put it on. They were in Max's little room in the back of Club Morgan and Shelley slid the ring onto her wedding finger and rose up in front of him naked. She was so thin and beautiful. Max felt he would cry from happiness. She waved her hands in the air so the ring could catch the light better and her hands became a kind of Balinese dance. I am yours, Shelley's dance said. I have given you everything and now I am yours. Max held out his hand to her to pull her back to the bed.

They were interrupted by a loud knock at the door.

Shelley froze and then tried to cover herself with her hands. Max couldn't believe this was really happening to him. He motioned to Shelley to make no sound. Maybe the crazy bastards would just go away. He pulled Shelley to him and she huddled against his chest.

"Open up! It's the police!"

"Holy Jesus!" Max said. "It's Bartleman!"

Shelley pushed him away roughly, gathered up her clothes and ran into the card room to get dressed.

"What the hell do you want, Bartleman?"

"Open this door. I want to talk to you."

"You got a search warrant?"

"You want me to break down this door?"

Max pulled his trousers on and opened the door. Bartleman hung in the doorway with his greasy fedora pulled down tightly on his bald head. He grinned when he saw Max standing bare-chested in front of him. Bartleman reeked of cheap, overripe rye.

"Hey, hey, hey," Bartleman said softly, as though he and Max were old friends, "you got a broadie in here!"

"Eat shit Bartleman. What do you want?"

"Me and you are going for a ride," Bartleman said. "Me and you have got things we should talk about."

Max wasn't afraid of Bartleman. He wasn't afraid of anyone if it came to that. It was just simpler to go along with the big detective. Max would get the cop out of the way and Shelley would be able to get home by herself. Bartleman drove him in an old black Ford to Cherry Beach and parked there. They became just one more anonymous car set incongruously among the couples who had come there to neck. A grain freighter, pale lights hanging from its masts, hooted its way cautiously toward the harbour. The sounds fell lonely and romantic over the lovers parked in the mist of Cherry Beach.

"Pretty out here, eh?" Bartleman said.

"Yeah, beautiful," Max said. "I bet it looks even better in daylight."

Bartleman handed him the mickey bottle and Max took a pull from it. The stuff burned his throat and made his eyes water. To Max, the cheap rye tasted and smelled like turpentine. Only a cop could drink such stuff.

"You ever wonder how Jake gets away with it? Besides his being a friend of mine," Bartleman said.

"Jake's smart," Max said.

"Horseshit," Bartleman said. "Jake can't hardly read. Don't you know that? He never even finished grade three. We let Jake go and we let a couple of other guys go as long as they don't get too big for their britches."

Max let that one go by and decided that Bartleman was probably being honest with him. From what Max had been able to learn from Jake, no one bookie was big enough to dominate all the action in town. It was humiliating to think there was an upper limit to how big Jake could get and that upper limit was set by the cops themselves.

"Guys come here all the time from the States," Bartleman said. "They think they're gonna be Al Capone. We educate 'em fast. Sometimes we have to take 'em down to the beach here and give them a swimming lesson."

Max felt suddenly very cold and vulnerable sitting in the car with Bartleman. He'd never thought much about it before but the cop must be six feet tall at least. And he sounded more than half drunk.

"Bartleman, what's this all about? You know Jake's operation. We're just trying to make a living."

"Jake's getting in with some bad actors," Bartleman said. "The Cleveland mob. We've been watching them. There's nothing goes on in this town that we don't know about, eh? If Jake don't cut it out, we're going to cut it out for him."

Bartleman spoke heavily, ponderously, like a judge reading a sentence. Max stayed quiet when he was finished, playing along with Bartleman, letting the words sink in. But underneath he was very excited. If Jake was going big, there would be something in it for him too. He wanted only to get away from Bartleman and ask Jake if the story was true. Maybe this would be the way out that he and Shelley had been looking for.

"So, you're gonna talk to Jake," Bartleman said. "And you're going to tell Jake to keep out of sight for a while."

"Come on, Bartleman, Jake isn't going to take that kind of stuff from me. You got something to say to Jake, so tell him yourself."

"Jake doesn't listen to me," Bartleman said. "Maybe we been friends too long. If Jake had listened to me, he wouldn't've wound up in the joint. Everybody in town knew he wasn't in on that bank job. Jake was just running a little crap game in those days. But we picked him up and he had some of the dough from the bank on him. I begged him. I pleaded with him, 'Your friends are running out on you, Jake,' I said to him. 'What the hell you want to worry about them for?' But Jake wouldn't say nothing. He took the fall himself. Jeezuss! Seven years in Kingston."

Max thought of Shelley going home alone from Club Morgan and he suddenly understood why the beautiful Nora loved Jake Besser and stayed with him. From time to time, pale, cold men showed up at the apartment and they sat alone with Jake, talking for hours. Nora never disturbed them but she told other people how there was no-one else in the world people trusted the way they trusted Jake. Seven years, Nora said, and Jake never opened his mouth. When he got out, everyone expected him to go after the guys who really did pull the bank job.

But Jake just laughed and went on about his business.

"Jake never bore a grudge and never hurt anyone," Nora always finished up. "Unless other people drove him into it."

Who could help but love a man as strong and as loyal as Jake Besser? An old line from a poem he had heard in high school came to Max: "Only the brave deserve the fair." On Berryman Avenue, only a man who could stand up for himself could hold the love of a woman like Nora. Or a woman like Shelley Englander.

"I'd like to help you, Bartleman," Max said. "But I just work for Jake."

"Jake thinks of you like his own kid," Bartleman said. "You're gonna tell him to keep away from Cleveland."

"Bartleman, how am I going to say anything like that to Jake? He'll kill me."

"I'm making you personally responsible for Jake Besser," Bartleman said. "You're a smart boy. You'll think of something to say."

Bartleman dropped him off in front of Steadman's. The sun was just beginning to come up and Max had a last cup of coffee while the waiters mopped the floor. Trucks bulging with fruit and vegetables and crates of live, squawking chickens nosed along the rows of gamblers' cars looking for places to park and unload. All his life Max had known this street but never before had he appreciated its complexities. So many different kinds of lives were going on here at the same time. Who could believe all the things that had happened to him in the last 24 hours? He thought of trying to explain it all to some of his boyfriends in Club Morgan. But, then, what would they think of Shelley? From now on he would have to keep his life more to himself. But he could talk to Shelley, at least. With her, there would be no secrets.

23

Max did pass on Bartleman's warning. It wasn't that he had any respect for the cop but he was worried about Jake. It was his duty to tell Jake what Bartleman had said. But Jake only laughed and all Max's fears were stilled. The cops were always trying to protect him, Jake said. If they protected him any more, he'd be six feet under.

Jake rented two rooms in the Cawthra Building and put a sign on the door, "Summerhill Social Club." Then the telephone company put in three phones, one of which was connected, as far as Max could tell, directly to every race track in the United States. Whenever Max called a certain number in Cleveland and asked for Mr. Pierce, Mr. Pierce came on the line and asked how the weather was in Toronto. And Max always said the weather at the Summerhill Social Club was just fine. And then Max was connected to the main line and a thick, nasal voice would come on announcing the latest races from tracks all over the United States — Santa Anita, Hialeah, Jamaica. The names of the winners and what they paid; Max wrote the results down on tiny slips of paper that could be easily torn up or even swallowed if the police suddenly showed up. Then Jake would get on the phone to his regular customers and tell them where they stood in his book, what they had won or lost. And did they want to bet some more?

The connection with Cleveland doubled and then tripled Jake's business. He had the fastest action in the city. Other bookies began calling to get the latest results and to lay off some of their heavier bets. Max found that he was out sometimes until two and three in the morning paying off and making collections. Sometimes he looked around and realized that Bartleman was following him in the old black Ford and he worried. Maybe they were getting too big too fast. Maybe the cops would get jealous and close them down. But Jake was too excited to listen to any talk of caution. The next step, he told Max, was they were going to rent a house just beyond the borders of the city, in Mimico, maybe, or New Toronto. They would have a big room with blackboards announcing the races from all over the country and guys could sit out there all day making bets. They would have card tables and crap games and who could tell? Maybe even some fancy stuff like roulette. The Summerhill Social Club was just the beginning, Jake said.

"I took a lot of hard knocks," Jake said. "When I come out of the joint, the depression was on already. Then there was the war. Everything was tight. You couldn't live. But now there's lots of money around. And a lot of guys are starting to make it big. So why not me? I got just as much right as they do."

In the fall, Max married Shelley Englander. He was drawing $200 a week from Jake and he had no longer any reason to fear for the future. The wedding took place in a rabbi's study, really just a cramped little office in the back of his house. Shelley brought a cousin to act as bridesmaid and Max brought two of his boyfriends from Club Morgan to be his best man and witness. They were the only people at the wedding. The ceremony lasted only 20 minutes and when it was over, the boys from Club Morgan put their suitcases in a car and drove Max and Shelley to Union Station. They took the train to Montreal for a four-day honeymoon. All the way there Shelley gazed out the window at the thick green fields of southern Ontario whizzing by her and she held tightly to Max's hand. She didn't let go of him even when they went into the dining-car for their wedding supper of roast beef and baked potatoes.

It was like one long party that first year. Max was the first of the boys to get married. He had rented an apartment on Bloor Street several blocks to the north of the hustle of Berryman Avenue, but still people were always dropping in on them. Max sometimes got annoyed but Shelley never minded. After the long, boring childhood in her father's house, her new life with Max was filled with laughter and excitement. Sometimes everybody took off from her apartment to a restaurant to have supper. Sometimes they just went down to the club to dance and play cards. The other girls asked her opinion and told her their problems. A married woman knew things they could only guess at. Some nights Max would come home late from his collections and there would still be people kibitzing around their kitchen table. Max and Shelley went to bed and just left them there. In the morning Shelley never minded cleaning up after them. She brought Max his coffee and his racing form in bed, and sat beside him rubbing his feet while he studied the morning line.

Neither the boys nor her own family ever spoke about what Max did for a living. Max had gone into the rackets and it was understood that a man who had gone into the rackets was involved in things he could not talk about. A couple of times a month, Shelley went home alone on Friday night for Shabbos supper. Her family never mentioned Max's name. It was as though she had no husband at all. The thought that Rochelle had married a gangster filled her father with grief. He sat at the head of the table, thrown into a dour silence whenever Shelley came. His sadness was so overpowering that hardly anyone else at the table had the courage to say anything either. Still Shelley was proud of the fact that she had not turned her back upon her family even if they were being so rotten to her she cried all night every time she visited them.

Lying beside her husband that summer on the hot, gaudy sand of Crystal Beach, Shelley marvelled at how much she had learned in a single year. She played with the thick black curls on Max's copper-coloured chest. He had filled out. He had a little moustache now and he was more watchful. Max didn't laugh as quickly or as loudly as he used to. He was changed completely from that trembling, angry boy she had allowed to undress her and force his way into her in the back room of Club Morgan little more than a year before. What a foolish, wild thing that had been to do. Thank God it had worked out for the best. She had thought then that she was just crazy about Max and would do anything he wanted. But only now, only after a year of marriage, was she really beginning to understand the meaning of love.

"Max, do you know what I want?" she said.

Max opened his eyes and saw her wide, rosy face above him.

"If we're going to stop using anything, I want to stop now, while we're here," Shelley said.

"It's up to you," Max said. "I don't know anything about kids. You're the one who's going to have to look after them."

"I'm ready," Shelley said. "I really want them now. I'm not afraid any more."

"Okay," Max said. "If it's what you want."

She kissed him then, right on the beach with all those millions of people around them. Max put his arms around her and she rested her warm head on his chest. Just holding her seemed to ease some of the pain and tension that Max felt. He decided not to discuss with her the business problems that were troubling him. After all, there was nothing she could do to help. But the truth was, the Summerhill Social Club was in deep trouble. And Max should not have been there, fooling around in Crystal Beach. He should have been back in Toronto helping Jake.

The trouble had begun over a month earlier. Two men had come to the door of the club early in the afternoon.

One of them was the handsomest man Max had ever seen. He wore a dark blue suit and his face was hard and burned red by the weather. He had thick grey hair too, and he might have been a famous soldier or a cowboy who had gotten rich and started his own ranch.

"I'm here to see Jake Besser," the man said politely. "Tell him it's John, out of Buffalo."

Jake went off with the man from Buffalo, leaving Max alone in the club with the second man who had come to the door. He looked to be about Max's age but thinner. His nose was big and hooked, more like a Jew's nose than a wop's, and his eyes were too close together. He looked almost cross-eyed. Max leaned against the wall, chewing on a toothpick and watched the wop walk about the silent, empty gambling club. The wop stopped by a table and idly fingered a pack of cards.

"You want a game?" Max said.

"Sure," the wop said. "Why not? We got lots a time. Two cents a point?"

"A nickel a point," Max said. "Let's make it interesting."

The wop leaned back in his chair and put his feet up on the table. The casualness didn't intimidate Max; it just annoyed him. This was a sloppy way to play gin rummy. Max filled his pipe with Old Chum tobacco and kept a steady stream of smoke going across the table.

"I know you," Max said, picking up the three of diamonds for his third gin.

"Yeah," the wop said. "I know you, too."

"Fulham Street Public School. You used to play hockey?"

"Yeah. I was on the Bantams when we won the whole city."

"That was a good team. Funny, eh?" Max said. "Your name's Mario, isn't it?"

"Bill," the wop said. He began to deal the cards. "My

28

name's Bill. I don't see many guys from the old school no more."

By the time Jake and the man from Buffalo came back, Max was ahead by 1600 points.

"I'll pay you tomorrow," Bill said.

"Forget it," Max said. "Just a friendly little game. Helps to pass the time."

When the two men had left the club, Jake exploded. Max had never seen him in such a state before. His face was bright throbbing red. He picked up a chair by the legs and marched back and forth in the club room. He was so mad he couldn't speak. He was gasping for air. Then he hurled the chair against the wall. Max stayed where he was, motionless at the card table. He was afraid to do anything else. Jake looked like he would kill anything that moved. Jake grabbed another chair and hurled it through the window. The sound was absurdly like tinkling Christmas bells. The chair seemed to hang for a moment and then toppled from the room. It fell on the alley side. Max said a silent prayer of thanks. Thank God Jake hadn't gone crazy in the front room. Just imagine a chair sailing through a window and landing in the middle of Berryman Avenue! Still, there could be people in the alley. There could be a cop. What would Bartleman do if he heard about it?

"They won't let you live!" Jake said quietly and he cursed them. "Fucking little cunts!"

He sat down at the table and Max quickly dealt him eleven cards. Jake picked them up automatically and began to study them. Through the window Jake had broken, sunlight poured into the stale air of the club. Max was astonished to see how bright and cheerful the sunlight was. It seemed like weeks since he had been out in the fresh air during the day.

"Couldn't we make a deal with them?" Max asked.

"Yeah, sure. We can make a deal," Jake said. "All they want is 50 per cent of our action, or they bring in their own wire. You want to give them 50 per cent of your pay?"

Without even thinking about it, Max said "No." Such a reduction was unthinkable. How could he cut in half the money he gave Shelley every week for the table?

So the decision was made and Max and Jake played gin rummy all that afternoon and never spoke again about what might happen to them in the future.

Business dropped off immediately. They had been using two people to man the phones while Max was on the wire to Cleveland, but the end of the second week Jake let them go. Max could handle all the action himself and still take the race results from Cleveland. By the end of the third week, all they had left was half a dozen regular players, old friends of Jake's. And even the old friends were not betting as much as they used to.

Jake stopped coming to the club. Max brought the money to his home every morning. His appearance shocked Max. He had never thought of Jake as an old man. But he found now that Jake was staying in bed all day and his voice was thin and quavering. His eyes seemed to be filling up with water all the time and his skin was so pale Max could see the purple veins. It was an old man's face.

Jake didn't fight back at all when Max told him that business was so slow he might as well go to Crystal Beach for a few days. Jake just nodded his head and Max felt like some kind of traitor turning on Jake. But there wasn't really anything for him to do at the club and Shelley needed a holiday.

When they got back, business was booming again. Max could hardly believe it. He felt his life was turning into a crazy roller-coaster ride. He wondered if he could take much more of this. One day, the club was so dead he could fall asleep in there. And the next day, the phone was ringing off the wall. All their old customers were back, and as Jake said, they brought their friends. Max tried to find out what had happened, but Jake said only "They took care of it on the other side. Everything is going to be hunky dory from now on."

Jake ordered himself three new custom-made suits at Weinstock's and gave Max a $500 bonus. Max took Shelley to New York. They stayed at the Algonquin Hotel and they saw Walter Winchell eating cheesecake at Lindy's. Shelley was astonished at how small and old he looked, as frail as her own grandfather. She told her friends she was surprised he could eat anything at all with all the people coming up to his table to talk to him. Max ordered breakfast in bed and they made love every morning with all the thrilling traffic of New York roaring and hooting outside their bedroom window. Max had never told Shelley anything about the troubles in the club. But he saw that she must have understood at least some of what was going on. She made love to Max now with a passion and a tenderness meant to tell him how sorry she was for all the grief she had caused by marrying him. In the late afternoons, Max sat up in bed smoking Lucky Strikes and reading the *Mirror* while Shelley dressed. Max marvelled at how many of the old things people used to pass off as wisdom turned out to be true. They used to say you didn't know how good it was until you had been sleeping with the same woman for a couple of years. Max always thought that was crazy. The more the merrier. But now he felt sorry for the poor guys still out there trying to hustle broads. What could they hope for? Ten minutes in and out if they were lucky. How could that compare with the long days he spent in bed with Shelley? Marriage was the true and natural state of man. There was nothing any woman in the world could do that his Shelley

31

couldn't do better. He took her to see Ethel Merman in *Annie Get Your Gun.* Sometimes the whole stage was filled up with singers and dancers all dressed up as cowboys and Indians but whenever Ethel Merman was on, she was the whole show. Max adored Ethel Merman. She was Jewish, and she was tough, and she was the toast of New York.

On Christmas Eve, the roof fell in. Max and Jake were coming out of Steadman's and six men jumped them with baseball bats. It had been a good week. All the regulars were trying to make their Christmas shopping money on the horses. Jake had a roll of over $10,000 in his pocket but the man who beat him didn't even bother to go through his pockets. They just attacked.

The first blow caught Max behind the knees and pitched him into the huge snow bank by the curb. He recognized Bill, the young Italian who had come to the club with the man from Buffalo. Bill brought the bat back as though he were calmly waiting for a pitch and then swung it into Max's ribs. The pain exploded in his chest but he didn't go out. He looked around and saw they hadn't got Jake down yet. There were four or five of them in a pack around Jake swinging the bats and Jake had his arms in front of his face trying to protect himself but he hadn't gone down. Max tried to get to his feet to help Jake but they hit him in the head. He turned and lunged for Bill but they kicked his legs out from under him. He fell to the sidewalk and they stood in a circle kicking him and hitting him with the baseball bat. All he could think about before he lost consciousness was that Shelley was keeping a late supper for him at home and nobody would call and tell her what had happened.

Nobody saw a thing. When Max came to, blood was trickling out of his mouth and he felt very stiff and cold. He knew that he had no power to move himself. They had taken his control of his life away from him. He lay still watching his blood float away and disappear into the black slush of Berryman Avenue until they came for him with a canvas stretcher and put him into an ambulance. The police swarmed up and down the avenue looking for witnesses but nobody remembered seeing anything. Even the people in Steadman's had not seen Max and Jake get beaten up right in front of the restaurant.

Johnny Bartleman came to see Max in the hospital. Max had four broken ribs and his front teeth had been knocked or kicked out. His thighs and stomach were covered with livid purple and yellow bruises.

"You want to tell us what's going on," Bartleman said to him. "Most of it we already know anyway."

"I don't know what's going on," Max said. "That's the honest truth. I don't know anything."

Bartleman was pleased by this answer.

"Aa-a-ah, you're Jake's boy all right," Bartleman said, and he left Max alone.

The hospital gave Max time to think about the future. It was months since he had had time to do anything but work. Jake had managed to talk his way out after a couple of days and Nora was looking after him at home. Max was all alone in this huge, sombre building downtown where nobody knew who he really was. Jake paid for a private room for him and Shelley came and sat with him every day. She read the newspapers to him and sat beside his bed holding his hand. She cried sometimes but she never spoke about what had happened and she never told Max what he ought to do.

When they finally let him out, Max went straight to Jake's apartment.

"It's got nothing to do with us," Jake said. "Some guys on the other side are having a fight, that's all. But they're getting it straightened out. You'll see. After the New Year, we'll be bigger than ever."

"Jake, let's go legit. We could make just as much money. And we wouldn't have this kind of *tsorres.*"

"What'll we do, open a cigar store? Or maybe sell fish? You want to open a fish store in the market?"

"There's lots of things we could do. But we got to start looking."

"You can't teach an old dog new tricks," Jake said. "Anyway, what do I want to go legit for? We're going to be the biggest bookmakers in the city."

"It's not worth dying for," Max said.

"What do you know about dying?" Jake said. "You don't know nothing about nothing."

There was a speech that Max Himmelfarb prepared but never delivered to Jake Besser. He tried to start it a couple of times but Jake always cut him short as though he already knew what Max was trying to say and didn't want to hear it. The speech was very important but the time for making it went by too quickly and Max never got a chance to tell Jake what he really felt. But if he had managed to say it to Jake, the speech would have gone something like this:

"I'm still young, Jake, and I don't have to live like this. I don't have to stay in the rackets because I don't know how to do anything else. I'm still young and I can go legit and make it on my own. I can make money and I can have a life where I don't have to keep looking over my shoulder watching out for guys with baseball bats. I'm young and, Jake, I'm strong enough for both of us. Maybe you're old but you're still smart. We can make a hell of a partnership. You can be legit and we can both be rich, Jake."

Max had a new bridge by the time they went to court. Looking at him, no-one could tell that all his bottom front teeth were false. Jake, because of his record, drew 90 days in the Don Jail. Bartleman had smashed down the door of the Summerhill Social Club and found Jake's daily record book. Jake and Max had been charged with keeping a common gaming-house. Max, because it was his first offence, got off with a fine. His brother-in-law Fred Englander was in the courtroom and Fred paid the fine on the spot, in cash. Max went to work for his father-in-law's company, Premier Paints. When Premier branched out into construction and then began to build whole shopping plazas and apartment blocks, Max Himmelfarb took on himself the job of assembling land. He was known for making sharp deals but Max was universally respected in the industry because he always kept his word. After the first boom, when Premier emerged from the real-estate jungle as one of the half-dozen largest real-estate developers in the country, the company was organized along more formal lines and Max Himmelfarb acquired the title of vice-president. He and Shelley bought a fifteen-room house on Old Forest Hill Road.

At the beginning of the sixties, Johnny Bartleman died. He was by then a deputy chief inspector and the newspapers were full of tributes to the famous detective. The police managed to keep the circumstances of Johnny's death away from the reporters. Only insiders knew that Bartleman had gone into his garage, closed the door tightly and started the motor of his new car. He had time to finish a mickey of rum and pack of cigarettes before the carbon monoxide neatly and painlessly put an end to all his troubles. Some people said that Johnny had been involved in too many goings-on and the young hotshots in the department were closing in on him. Others said he was just getting old and despondent. He was certainly alcoholic in his last years.

Jake Besser was an honorary pallbearer.

Max Himmelfarb didn't even make it to the funeral. He was in Montreal that day, at the Royal Bank, arranging to borrow from a consortium of lenders $27 million to finance Englishtown, the largest apartment complex ever built in Canada.

Toronto, 1977

Marvin, Marvin

We knew Jake Wells for almost twelve years and at least one of us knew her completely. But in the end, it turned out that we knew hardly anything at all about her. Or, for that matter, about ourselves.

We first met Jake Wells the summer the Greenie's father bought the baby-blue Chrysler. The old man couldn't drive, but after Hungary and the war, I guess he wanted to buy something to show that he had finally made it to safety. So his son, the greenhorn, our Greenie, sixteen years old and still gaunt and pock-marked with acne, still ready to claw and bite anyone who questioned him, had a huge powerful blue car and a radio that could pick up Minneapolis late at night to play with. The old man would come to the curb in front of his Budapest Authentic Dairy restaurant and wave to us as we drove off.

At first, it was just trips to Hamilton to get a cup of coffee, but we didn't know anybody in Hamilton so we moved on to Niagara Falls and then Buffalo. But we didn't know anyone in Buffalo either and the Chrysler wasn't as much help as we'd thought it was going to be. There were more Chryslers in Buffalo than in Toronto. We'd park the car and walk up and down Main Street and Delaware Avenue, watching all the Americans go by and trying to work up enough nerve to speak to them. But they were all so glossy, like magazine ads, like people out of teenage movies, that we always hung back, laughing and snarling among ourselves. People in Buffalo seemed to know so much more than we did. We'd see people who were maybe the same age as us, but they looked older, and when we were close enough to hear them, sounded so much smarter and more sure of themselves. We called them conformists and American fascists and we hid out in the safety of the Greenie's Chrysler.

We'd sit in the car sneering at them and speculating on which of those girls floating past our fish-tank windows was going to get laid that night. Finally, the Greenie, in his abrupt way, would wheel the car into the parking-lot of the Robin Hood Restaurant and we'd know that the night was over except for the last cup of coffee and the long ride home up the Queen Elizabeth Highway listening to Phil MacKellar play Sauter-Finnegan records. Songs were meant to sing, ah, but Nina never, Nina never, Nina never knew. . . .

We drove to Buffalo every Saturday and sometimes

Friday night too that spring. There was the Greenie,
Herbie Applebaum, Marv Wise and myself. We had just
finished grade twelve and as far as we were concerned, high
school was already over. But we still had one more year to
go before we could get into university and we knew and
accepted that it was going to be a bitch. Herbie and Marv
were planning for medical school but the old Jewish quota
that nobody had ever proved but which we all knew
existed, meant that they had to get at least six first-class
honours, at least two more than the average goy, to get in.
I only had to get 60 percent to get into an arts course and
go on to law and the Greenie was still talking about getting out of this shitty country and going back to Europe.
Grade thirteen was just the final insult from the system,
the last spiteful clearing of the throat by the pasty, chalk-
dusted bastards.

Our consuming hatred of the fat, comfortable, rich,
smug school we went to welded us together. No-one else
talked to us. Other people at Shalmar Road Collegiate, the
ones who went to each other's parties every weekend and
belonged to fraternities and had gold pins to hang on the
fifteen-year-old bosoms of their steadies, looked upon us as
a quartet of sour, sarcastic misfits. We went only to western
movies on the weekends and until the principal himself,
no less, ordered us to cut it out, we brought copies of
Playboy to read ostentatiously in the school cafeteria every
day. The girls thought we were vulgar and maybe a little
dangerous. We talked too much and we dressed badly. The
boys believed we were unsporting and probably unmanly.
The four of us were lousy basketball players. I suppose the
fact that we were so far beyond the pale of civilized society
drew us to Jake Wells.

We met her on a weekend in July when we had gone up
to Camp Northern Pine to visit Marv. He had taken a job

39

as canoe instructor and since part of his job was to send kids out on canoe trips, he had charge of the sleeping-bags and on the weekends when we came out to visit him, he made us a little camping spot. The second time we came, we found him sitting in front of a fire he had made to welcome us, drinking cocoa with Jake Wells.

As things later worked out, I think I got to know her better than anyone except maybe the Greenie. And I don't think she was ever more beautiful than she was at seventeen. Later, she lost a little weight and learned how to dress and do things with her hair, but when she was seventeen she was short and soft and round. A mediaeval page-boy. A collector of stray cats and later stray people. A nymph, a fox, a butterfly. Virginal, but neither proud nor coy about it, she could still remember when boys had been only other people and she still wanted to be friends with them. When the time came, she would pick one of them. The time was almost on her. We could smell it. An odour of face powder and wet wool rolled off Jake in delirious waves. Her voice was soft, almost a whisper, but with an attractive, deep hoarseness to it and her eyes were brown and grave.

Marv wasn't at all happy to see us that first night. He told us later he'd been having a serious talk with Jake and nobody could talk about anything serious with the Greenie around snorting and hooting. Jake had become Marv's special buddy at Camp Northern Pine. They sat on the camp dock together at night, watching the moon and listening to the loons while they talked about life and what they wanted from the world. Marv swore to us that he hadn't laid a finger on Jake, that she was just a friend. He was just trying to help her solve her problems, Marv said.

The next day was Marv's day off and we found out all about Jake Wells. We'd come to take Marv for a drive around the Muskoka Lakes in the Greenie's car and Jake

40

came too. We found out that her right name was Jacqueline Welinsky and that her father was a doctor in Buffalo and she'd come to a camp in northern Ontario to get so far away that he'd never have time to visit her. Her father was always telling her how to run her life. She wanted to be an artist and he wanted her to marry a nice boy and settle down in an apartment house he owned. We'd all heard stories like this before; almost all the girls we knew had father problems, just as the boys had mother problems. But we felt somehow that Jake was going to put up a fight for what she wanted and we all did our best to be sympathetic to her. Her sister was a social worker. Her brother was at Annapolis, Jake said, and he was a prick. Locked in the Greenie's car with her, we all tried to pretend we were unimpressed. But underneath, we were shocked. We all knew that girls used dirty words when they were alone, but we'd never heard one swear in front of boys before.

We went to Buttermilk Falls. It was really just a dam and a stretch of boiling rapids between a couple of Muskoka Lakes, but there was a beach and some tourist cottages and a few stores. Jake sat on the shore talking to Marv and drawing in her sketch pad while Herbie, the Greenie and I plunged into the water. We swam so far out into the lake that Marv and Jake seemed to melt into the huge granite boulders on the shore. But we could feel them watching us and we were terribly pleased. We all felt that somehow we'd made it. At last, we had one of them with us. Jake was a girl from Buffalo. Maybe we'd even seen her that spring tripping along Delaware Avenue in the sparkling seven o'clock dusk with boxes under her arm, on her way home to dress for a party we hadn't been invited to.

We swam so far into the lake I began to worry about getting back. The Greenie turned around; he never took an uncommercial risk even then, but Herbie and I kept going and I wouldn't stop before he did. The water had been cold at first and then warmed up as we got used to it. But now the cold was beginning to get to me again. It seemed to seep right through to my bones. But my arms reached ahead in long looping strokes. I grew warm again; I became a machine; I was invincible. I began to feel I could swim on like this forever, watching the line of fir trees on the far shore bob and sink and bob up again as I drew closer to them, inching my way ahead through the lonely black water.

When Herbie and I got back, we found the Greenie sitting by himself on the branch of a tree. Jake and Marv had stopped talking to him. The Greenie had watched them sketch the lake and then announced that Jake was a lousy artist. She drew everything small and stiff, he said. Her drawings looked like she had constipation. Marv had told him to mind his own damned business and the Greenie had climbed the tree and watched for us. Herbie and I immediately joined him in the attack.

We told Jake she was a parasite. She was living in luxury while people in Africa and Asia were starving. Americans were all fascist bastards. They needed a father figure like Eisenhower to tell them what to do and a comic book like *Time* magazine to make the world simple for them. Jake said she'd never heard anybody in Buffalo talk like us and she wanted to know if we were Communists. No, we told her, but we would be if we lived in Cuba or Algeria or someplace like that. In Canada, we were socialists. We'd all gone knocking on doors for the CCF in the last election. Socialism could save the world if only the goddamned Americans would give it a chance. But the Americans were too greedy. They wanted to squeeze the last dime out of every country they could. They refused to let people in other countries decide their own fate and run their own lives. Everyone in the outside world was just like us, we assured her. Everyone hated Americans. McCarthy was going to take over the country. It was doomed. Jake was doomed. It was the last days of the Roman Empire. When we had done enough, we stopped. When we had Jake so bewildered and angry she didn't know whether to sing "The Star Spangled Banner" or burst into tears, we knew we'd won. We were very proud and pleased. We finally had a girl from Buffalo all to ourselves and we'd beaten her right into the ground.

Marv had stolen some food from the camp's tripping supplies, and we made a fire and roasted hotdogs and marshmallows. To make our peace with Jake, we told funny stories about the crazy teachers in our school. We sat for a long time in silence too, watching the bright red sparks shoot up and die. The four of us felt very close; we were brothers and Jake was becoming one of us. We even sang a little. The darkness hid our faces and made our voices sound less artificial. Herbie, who had a fine tenor, led us in "Mountain Greenery" and "Some Enchanted Evening." Marvin and Jake had to be in camp at eleven o'clock and we drove them back. At the gate, Jake kissed us all on the cheek and made us promise to come to Buffalo to see her.

In the next year, only Marv did. We were all too busy trying to get ourselves through grade thirteen to think about anything else. Besides, in October, the Greenie smashed up the Chrysler so badly his father had to sell it for junk and the old man refused to buy another one. So we were reduced to going to the movies again on Saturday nights, tramping home through the snow and spring slush promising each other how much better the world was going to be once we got into university. But Marv had an aunt in Buffalo and he hitch-hiked over a couple of times during the year to stay with her and see Jake. And I suppose it was partly because of him that Jake was waiting for us when we finally took that long bus and subway ride down to the University of Toronto.

Herbie enrolled in Meds but Marv had made only three firsts and had to go into Dents. I decided to take a straight three-year BA because I wanted to get into law school as quickly as possible. The Greenie surprised us all by registering in the school of architecture. We'd been waiting a long time to come downtown and the size and complexity of the university never bothered us. The boys and girls who'd been on the student council of Shalmar Road Collegiate and had run the prom committee and the social life of the school as though it was a feudal empire, all faded out in university. They'd grown too accustomed to having everything handed to them just because they dressed neatly and smiled all the time, even in their sleep. The year the university got us, it also got a new president, Claude T. Bissell. In his opening speech to the students, Bissell announced that he wasn't interested in the well-rounded man. He wanted people who were "angular." Nobody had more rough edges than we did and we prospered.

All by himself, the Greenie organized a sculpture club and bullied somebody on the campus into giving him money for clay and life models. I started doing book and movie reviews for the *Varsity* and that was the beginning of my undoing. Herbie joined the debating union and eventually became a star basketball player for the Blues, and Marvin became one of the boys on campus. The first year pre-Dents course bored him. There were too many books on it that he'd already read and in the science courses, there was too much trivia that he couldn't see being of much use to him in the business of fixing people's

44

teeth. Marvin spent most of his time drinking beer and just sitting in the Arbor Room at Hart House with a full cup of coffee in front of him. He wanted to find some real life, he said. The university was more of a cocoon than high school had been. He was the person we always called on Thursday nights to find out where the parties were going to be on the weekend.

All four of us paid court to Jake Wells. She had come to Toronto to make herself into an artist. Jake burned to be an artist. She was going to get it all down on canvas, everything that was going on inside her. Nobody had ever painted the soul of a woman, she said. She was going to be the first. I went once to take her home from a life drawing class and found her working on a nude. The model was a huge woman with pink splotches on her skin, lying on a dusty brown couch. I was fascinated by her crotch. The patch of long, ragged hair looked more like the chest of a gorilla than the object of all my fevered imaginings. I couldn't take my eyes off it.

"Go away, for God's sake," Jake hissed at me. "Everybody's looking at you."

"I just want to watch you work a little," I said. "Every artist needs a little criticism from outside now and again."

"You're a dirty old man," Jake said.

But there wasn't much sex in Jake's drawing of the woman. In fact, there wasn't much of anything. The charcoal lines were clean and neat. They rendered faithfully all the details of the woman. But it might have been a drawing of a corpse. There was no life in it, nothing original or striking. I felt a kind of pity for Jake. She had good taste but no particular talent. She was a product of the great culture boom. For Jake, art was a cause. To call herself an artist was to proclaim that she was more sensitive, better educated and, above all, less interested in money than her parents had been.

"Without art, I'd shrivel up," Jake explained to me later while she cooked us dinner in her apartment. "Even if I'm not a genius, I have to keep painting. Otherwise I'd be nothing. Don't you see that?"

"Why can't you just look at it?" I said. "Find out all you can about art. Learn how to really appreciate what you're looking at. Make yourself into an expert."

"If I have to, I will," Jake said. "But right now, that's not enough for me. I want the real thing. I'm going through an idealistic stage. I want to express myself."

"The road to hell is filled with people expressing themselves," I said.

"Shut up and eat," Jake said. She shoved a plate of hamburger and boiled potatoes in front of me. "God what a mean little prick you're going to be when you grow up."

Jake's apartment was absurdly expensive and overlooked my old high school. But she'd managed to convince her father that it was safer for her to live there than around the campus after the university women's residence had kicked her out. Jake had used the residence as just a place to sleep between her art classes. She hadn't even bothered registering in any university lectures. When the dean of the women's residence found out what she was up to, Jake got a week's notice to get out.

"It's marvellous," Jake said. "Nobody cares what time I get in at night or what time I get up in the morning. Nobody in this whole apartment building even knows I'm here, except for the superintendent and he never bothers me. For the first time in my life, I'm free and independent. Oh, God, that makes me feel so good."

"What surprises me is your old man," I said. "After everything you've told me about him, I mean."

"He thinks I'm living with two other girls," Jake said.

46

I kicked off my shoes, stretched out on the couch and pulled Jake down on top of me. Kissing Jake was an experience in itself. She tried to suck you dry. She fastened her lips on you and dug her fingers into your shoulders and scratched your neck, and hung onto you until you were gasping for breath and finally you had to push her away. When you looked at her eyes, you saw that they were out of focus and woolly and Jake was sweating and ready for it. She let me take everything off her except her underpants. They were always cotton, opaque, usually white and very brief and thin. But she would never let me take them off her or even put my hand inside them.

"I'm not saving myself for my husband and I don't have any big thing about virginity," Jake said. "It's just that I don't think you really know what you're doing. You want to take my pants off just because I want to keep them on. And that's not good enough for me. When I decide to give myself to someone, really give myself I mean, I'll choose the time and the place and the person."

Jake was right of course. She read less and worried less than we did, but she always seemed to be just that little bit ahead of us. We wouldn't really have known what to do if Jake had decided to let one of us make love to her. But Marv, Herbie, the Greenie and I all tried during that year to get Jake. She kept us all at a distance and she kept the Greenie farther away than anyone else. But we kept coming back for more; buying her suppers or buying the wine when she cooked in her apartment and taking her out to movies and art shows. I don't think we would ever have allowed any other girl to treat us as cavalierly as Jake did. But she had already become a kind of special person for us.

We wrestled on her couch until the sky outside the window was already beginning to wash out into the pre-dawn grey, and then we fell asleep together. Sometime later, so softly I didn't even feel her get up, Jake put on her long flannel nightgown and snuggled back beside me. In the morning, I stood in my stocking feet on her balcony and listened to the bells ring in my old school and heard the muffled sound of the students marching through the halls to change their classes. I could hardly believe that barely six months before, my life too had been organized and controlled by those bells, and that now I was standing, bleary-eyed and unshaven and gloriously free on Jake's balcony. She brought me a cup of coffee. It seemed I had never risen so late before on a school-day morning. It was a grainy November morning, wet and dark with approach of winter. The streets were almost empty. People were already at work, busy doing and being. I could see down over the roofs of the city to the neon sign on the roof of the Park Plaza Hotel. I drank Jake's coffee and I felt myself growing older and tougher and wiser. The world looked very good from the balcony of Jake's apartment.

Jake and the apartment went at the end of February. Her father came to visit her in Toronto and saw how she was living. He packed Jake up and drove her home. It cost the old boy two months' rent but I guess he thought it was worth it to save his daughter from a life of sin—or at least a life of art. We all kept in touch with Jake through letters and at least a couple of times a year in the years that followed, she came to Toronto and stayed at Marv's with his mother acting as chaperone. Seeing Jake was always a pleasure. We measured ourselves against her and usually discovered that no matter what we'd learned in the time since we'd last seen her, she still knew a little bit more than we did.

Marvin was the first among us to get laid for real. Her name was Kathleen and only her analyst knows why she latched onto Marvin. Kathleen was a 35-year-old divorcée.

48

For a living, she was a nurse at the Toronto Women's Hospital. For kicks, she kept a chintzed-up, brass four-poster bed in a bachelor apartment on St. George Street. Kathleen had bright yellow hair fluffed around her bony little face like scrambled eggs and the biggest bosom I've ever seen. Mostly, she covered it with tight black sweaters but sometimes she did us all a favour and showed up in a black cocktail dress scooped out to just barely above her navel. The game at our table in the KCR then was to try and make Kathleen laugh in the vain hope that her tits would pop right out of the dress. They never did, of course. But at least when she laughed, she rocked back and forth and we could cast guarded little glances at the freckled beginnings of her huge tits and sometimes even see down into the black-ribbed, shadowy mysteries of her body. And seeing Kathleen's tits in those days was almost —although we never pretended it was anything more than almost—as good as fucking her.

The King Cole Room was our place. On rare occasions, an essay or a test completed, a freshman girl we were trying to impress, we took the rocket elevator up to the seventeenth floor and the glossy, glassy, rooftop bar of the Park Plaza. But on the roof, we considered it beneath our dignity to drink anything less than scotch and water. Unfortunately, what we got for weekly allowance from our parents didn't allow us that sophistication very often. It galled us to be taking money from our parents but we were still students and, as we saw it, we were caught in an impossible trap. We had to spend a reasonable number of hours every day in classes and libraries and to take a part-time job meant eating into our drinking time. So we took enough money from our fathers to buy draft beer in the King Cole Room and pretend that we were really poor.

The King Cole Room was a vast, lunar cave that used to

exist in the bowels of the Park Plaza. Some of the walls were hung with little triangles and circles that always reminded me of the lobby of a movie palace built in the thirties. The rest of the walls were smoked-glass mirrors. Under the flickering lights, the mirrors tinted the drinkers with a grey pallor that made them look physically as well as emotionally sick. But the darkness was a kind of balm too; you could hide in it and be healed. You could drink for hours at a crowded table and still be utterly alone, cut off by the shadows and bars of faint light. And other times, if it was a good night, a kind of warmth grew up under the icy walls and ceiling. People called to each other, chairs were pulled together and the whole KCR became one vast table brimming with talk and hysterical laughter.

At first, Kathleen was just another face swimming up out of the silvery gloom to join us. Then, somehow, by some subtle process of chemistry, she became Marvin's special friend. In the hoarse, glassy-eyed camaraderie of the long nights in the KCR, I didn't realize how involved Marvin had become until I got a letter from Jake. She wanted to know why nobody was coming to see her any more and why no-one was even writing to her. I went looking for Marvin. I found him in the Honey Dew on Bloor Street with a huge, fifteen-cent mug of coffee. He clutched the mug with both hands as though he were an elderly refugee and the coffee his first food in three days.

"I'm in love with Kathleen," he said.

"Sure you are."

"I want to marry Kathleen."

"A fine idea. Take her home tonight to meet your mother."

"My mother thinks I'm going to Buffalo every weekend to see Jake," Marvin said. "I leave home Friday, sometimes even Thursday and I don't come back till Sunday night.

My mother never says anything. She's hoping I'll settle down with Jake but she's afraid to push me. Crazy, isn't it?"

"Probably," I said. "But you're the envy of your friends, if that's any comfort to you."

"We're sensible people," Marvin said. "We're not supposed to get involved in things like this."

"We're middle-class people. Love in moderation and everything else in its own good time and place."

"I'll have to quit school," Marvin said. "Kathleen could support me, but I don't want her to. It would be too much like still getting an allowance. I can get a job in a dental lab. I'm good with my hands. And I like it better than looking down people's throats all day."

"You've really got it all worked out, eh?"

"We make plans," Marvin said. "We don't let things just happen to us. We're sensible people."

Marvin looked dirty. He had always had a heavy beard, but now his whole face seemed to be coming out in grimy steel wool. His chicken-fat cheeks had caved in; his skin had the mealy white colour and texture of gefilte fish. Dandruff scales glinted in the curly black skullcap that was Marvin's hair. Even his clothes looked bedraggled. Marvin's college uniform, day, night and festive occasions, was a pair of charcoal-grey slacks and a maroon windbreaker with "Dentistry" embroidered on the back in grey script. Now the jacket was wrinkled and smudged with black and brown stains, as though Marvin had been sleepng in a ditch for several weeks.

"Marvin," I said. "Marvin, you're going to have to do something about this."

"Like what?"

"Like get out. Like get a grip on yourself."

"You wouldn't talk like that," Marvin said, "if it had ever

happened to you. You don't understand. You don't know what it's like."

"Touché," I said. "One for you. So I'm still a virgin, technically at least."

"It's not just getting laid," Marvin said. "Anybody can do that."

"I'm having my troubles."

"I believe in love," Marvin said. "Does that sound crazy to you?"

"Sort of," I said.

"If you love someone you ought to be home free," Marvin said. "The two of you can get away and make a life for yourselves. You don't need anyone else. You don't have to worry any more about what people think of you. You just get away with the one person you care about and you can tell all the stupid things in the world to go to hell. That's what I want to do with Kathleen; set things up so the two of us can have our own private little world."

"What does Kathleen think about all of this?"

"She says her marriage was like being in jail. Now she wants some fun out of life."

"Is that what you want too?"

"For now," Marvin said. "For a while, anyway. It's interesting. It's a good life, once you get used to it. But people like you and me, we weren't cut out to go on like this indefinitely. We're sensible people."

I went to the counter and got us two more mugs of coffee. It was a bitter January day. The streets were like the bones of a skeleton, bleached white by the cold. The antiseptic old Honey Dew became a cozy haven. Marvin and I sat together through the afternoon. We talked about Herbie and the Greenie and what would happen to us all in the end. We worked through love and sex to philosophy and we cursed life. How could one be sensitive, important,

52

alive, in Toronto? The city was the original backwater of western civilization. Toronto was where they would put the pipe if they wanted to give the world an enema. But we were Torontonians and even the sound of the word had a pompous, artificial ring to it. And the people who were on television and radio or who wrote newspaper columns, or who got themselves written up by the columnists, all tried to carry on as though they were real celebrities. But their voices always sounded hollow and phoney. They were giggling in public to keep their courage up. The fact that they had never been, nor would they ever be, heard of beyond the suburbs of the city seemed somehow to have penetrated those painted wooden heads. And we, Marvin and I, we ended by agreeing that no matter how big we became, no matter what we did or how wildly we loved, as long as we were in Toronto, we would always be small-time. As the supper crowd began to fill the Honey Dew, Marvin wound his scarf around his neck and zippered up his windbreaker. He hadn't had such a good talk since leaving high school, he said. He shook my hand, an oddly formal thing to do. Old friends should get together more, he said. Then he disapeared into the six o'clock blackness of Bloor Street. He was walking down to the hospital to meet Kathleen.

Kathleen, it turned out, was able to keep it up much longer than Marvin. She'd had more practice at it. Marvin took to spending whole weeks instead of just weekends at her apartment. Sometimes he'd arrive there and find her so full of dope she could hardly recognize him. She was getting pot and hashish from the orderlies in the hospital and she kept it in a Chinese porcelain tea canister beside her bed with a little yellow package of Vogue cigarette papers. She tried rolling some for Marvin but he never mastered the trick of inhaling, and the stuff didn't do much for him.

He stuck to Teacher's Highland Cream and although they each got high in their separate ways, they stayed up there together for days on end. The only time they came out of the apartment was for food — Kathleen kept only soda water, tangerines and Estonian black bread in her fridge— or to join a table in the KCR.

But even when they came to drink beer and talk to people besides each other, they hardly said a word. And nobody spoke to them. Marvin and Kathleen were isolated by the romantic grandeur of the scene they were making together. They were ghosts at the bachelor feast. Marvin looked pale and aesthetic. You half expected him to leap onto a table and begin reciting his latest poem. Kathleen's bosom seemed to be growing. Or maybe it was just she was losing weight and her boobies protruded more. Her eyes protruded too. They rolled around like mad, bloodshot ball bearings. Morning-glory seeds had just arrived in town as the newest kick and Kathleen baked cookies encrusted with them. I began to wonder how Kathleen managed to survive at the hospital. I feared for the lives of the patients there if she had to stick needles into them. She was all right, calm and serene, looking perpetually half asleep as long as Marvin was with her. But if he had to leave for any reason, she panicked. She clutched his sleeve and made him explain where he was going and how long would he be there and he had to promise to rush back to her side.

"He's beautiful, isn't he?" she said to me once while we were waiting for Marvin to come back from the men's room at the KCR.

"Marvin's a fine person," I said. "One of the best."

"Such broad shoulders," Kathleen said. "You wouldn't believe it just to look at him, but when he takes off his shirt, he's like a bull."

"I just had a brilliant idea," I said. I was onto my seventh or eighth beer. The night was long; the world was beautiful.

"I'm not ready for marriage," Kathleen said. She drew back from me as though afraid I was going to slap her face.

"You could do worse than Marvin," I said. "He's a great guy. He's my best friend."

"I'm in love with Marvin," Kathleen said. "Isn't that enough?"

"It's enough for me," I said. "Marvin may be a little harder to please."

"I don't want any trouble," Kathleen said. "No big scenes. No hangups. Marvin's here, you understand? That's the most important thing about him. Marvin's here and I'm here and we're doing fine. We're getting a lot of kicks out of just being together. If tomorrow I go someplace else or if Marvin goes someplace else, nobody's hurt. We say goodbye and that's that. We never had anything so we can't lose anything. It's life."

"Here's to life," I said.

We clinked our glasses and watched Marvin fight his way through the crowds back from the can.

"Here's to life," Kathleen said. "You want to know something? Until this moment I used to think you were a snotty little prick, but now I like you."

That was the last serious conversation I had with Kathleen. She and Marvin faded out of polite society. He moved a suitcase of clothes to her apartment and just stayed there. Kathleen went to the hospital every morning at six and then Marvin padded around the apartment reading back copies of the *Canadian Medical Association Journal* and the *Reader's Digest*. Some days, he didn't even bother to put any clothes on. He'd be sitting in an easy chair naked when Kathleen came home at four o'clock with the groceries and more whisky. Marvin cooked meals for them and washed the dishes himself. Then they lay on the bed watching the early movie on television until they had drunk enough and smoked enough to get high and then they would roll toward each other and flop into position, click, bang, bang, bang until Kathleen's alarm clock turned them off in the morning.

Later, when he talked about that time in Kathleen's apartment, Marvin called it an idyll. It was the high point of his life. "Whole days went by and I never saw daylight," he said. "It was like being in a cave. And no matter how much we did, I never got tired. I could go on all night and sometimes all day too, and I could always get it up one more time. I began to think I must be a special person. God must be watching and blessing me, I thought. I'm not a religious person but there are times when you think you must be getting a reward you don't really deserve and you've got something extra, something you can't explain, going for you."

Marvin made only one mistake. He went home for a week. He had intended going for only a couple of hours to pick up some clean clothes but he fell asleep at his mother's kitchen table. He was drinking coffee with her, and he just passed out, still sitting up. His mother insisted he go to bed and stay there. The doctor said it was nothing serious. Marvin was just overtired; he'd probably been studying too much. Marvin's mother fed him bowls of vegetable soup and when she was out of the room, he called Kathleen. Over the telephone, she was casual and gay. Marvin never suspected what was happening.

When he finally escaped from his mother, he went straight to Kathleen's. He knocked on the door, but no-one came to open it. He pounded on the door, but still there was no answer. He thought perhaps Kathleen had taken so much dope that she was in a stupor. He went down to the KCR, had a couple of beers and started phoning her. He called her three times and the last time, he let the phone ring for half an hour. Then he went back to her apartment. He found his suitcase sitting on the rubber welcome mat.

"I went crazy," he told me later. "I tried to bust the door down. It wasn't so much the idea of Kathleen getting rid of me. I could understand that. I was more serious than she really wanted to be. But I knew she had another man in there. That really killed me. I couldn't stand the idea of somebody else already being in that bed and me standing there in the hall like an idiot, locked out. I screamed at her and kicked the door. Then I went to the end of the hall and ran at it. It's a wonder I didn't break my shoulder. People started popping out of the other apartments and staring at me. They must have thought I was a first-class nut. I got worried that somebody would call the cops, so I just sat down beside my suitcase. I knew Kathleen had to go to the hospital in the morning and I figured I'd wait her out. I smoked a whole package of cigarettes and then I got scared. I was afraid of what would happen if Kathleen really did come out of the apartment and I was still there. I didn't want her to see me like that. So I took my suitcase and went home. The sun was already up when I left."

"You're lucky you got out of it so easily," I said.

"You live, you learn," Marvin said. "I'd still like to know what I did wrong."

"Sounds like you're ready for another round."

"No," Marvin said. "No. It's over. I wouldn't go back now, even if she asked me to. Enough is enough."

But Kathleen did call him again and he did go back to her. It was in the spring and Marvin should have stayed in the library studying for his exams, but Kathleen said she was alone and frightened and she needed him. It didn't last long. They spent more time fighting than doing anything else. Things about Kathleen that Marvin had never even noticed before suddenly irritated him beyond bearing. Once he told her, ordered her, to wash the underwear that she had piled up in a corner of the bathroom, and she threw a clock at him. Marvin grew to hate the apartment and he took to going for long walks in the afternoon. Kathleen was furious when she called from the hospital and he wasn't there to answer the telephone. At the end of three weeks, Marvin packed his suitcase and went home again.

Marvin didn't even try to get his year. After he left Kathleen, he sat in the KCR until the end of April and then he got a job manning the telephone in a real-estate office. His mother talked to him, Herbie talked to him, I talked to him, even the Greenie talked to him, and he told us all to leave him alone. Finally I wrote to Jake and Jake wrote to him and he went to see her in Buffalo. Jake was too full of her own troubles to waste much time trying to talk Marvin into going back to school. She was in the middle of her first honest-to-God love affair and she and Marvin discovered they had a lot in common. They sat up all weekend talking about Life and what they wanted from other people. When he came back to Toronto, Marvin applied to re-enter Dentistry. They made him beg for it. He hadn't written any of his exams and as far as the school was concerned, he was a dangerous element. But he pleaded with them and got his own personal dentist to write them a letter and finally the school allowed him to come back on the understanding that he was on probation until Christmas. A chance was all Marvin needed. He finished the year third in his class and when he graduated a couple of years later, he won a scholarship to study orthodontics in Syracuse.

The University of Toronto made us. I can hardly

remember now what we were like before we went there. We were sleepwalkers when we went into the machine; we'd been machine-tooled, coloured-in and given landscapes to operate in by the time we came out the other end. The Greenie never did finish architecture. He didn't have to. He started sculpting full time, moulding clay and bits of driftwood he found along the shore of the Muskoka Lakes. He grew a pencil-thin moustache and set himself up in the apartment over the old man's dairy restaurant as "Zoltan, Sculptor." I told him it sounded like "Zoltan, Man of Steel," but the Greenie knew what he was about. He screwed lightbulbs into some of the driftwood and sold it as lamps. Zoltan, the sculptor, four-button, plum-velvet suits and suddenly his accent, the "Zo, what kind difference makes it?" that we'd been making fun of for years, was very much in style. The Greenie made more in a week than I did in a month.

But he was more than this, more than the whisky-sipping, wild-dancing, hand-kissing and mildly insulting lapdog that he let the people who bought his lamps in Eaton's and came around to buy his "serious works" think he was. He kept his really serious works in a locked room and for a long time, only a couple of us ever saw them. He was still the refugee, too proud, too arrogant to give anyone the chance to criticize him. When he finally did take the good stuff out of his closet and put it into a one-man show, I drove him to Huntsville and back on opening night. We rolled into Toronto at eight o'clock in the morning and pounded on the gallery door until we got the gallery owner to open up. He slept on a cot in the back. He was the same age as us but he wore a beard that made him look younger. He opened the gallery door and gave us hell. Artists just have to attend opening nights! he said. That was how this business worked and we'd damned well better learn that! Who the hell did the Greenie think he was? Picasso or something? Three cases of Canadian champagne and no artist to pour it for the paying customers! If the customers can't touch the artist, they won't put out money for his stuff. Never let it happen again, the gallery owner shouted. Or you can find someone else to peddle your goddamned hunks of wood.

But he turned most of his anger on me. He was already afraid of the Greenie, afraid of losing him. The Greenie's "Congruencies," as he called them, had been too big a success. In a way, the Greenie's art was an insult to the people who bought it. They were mostly middle-class, middle-aged people who believed in the rule of law and the essential goodness of of humanity. The Greenie's work was inhuman. He took the driftwood, sanded away all the rough spots and finally painted it. All that remained was the grotesque shape. The Greenie removed or disguised everything natural to the wood. Then he took his weird painted shapes and strung them together with bits of plastic, coloured glass, rusty sheets of iron and unfinished cement to make five- and six-foot-high sculptures. They were harsh, bitter things to look at but they held the eye. If they had any message at all to deliver—and the Greenie hypocritically claimed they didn't—it was that beauty as something that elevated the soul was as dead as God. The Greenie's art was a proclamation of ugliness and anarchy.

But it sold. It sold for outrageous prices and the Greenie became a statistic in the great Canadian art boom. It wasn't quite like the ugly duckling. He was still capable of startling cruelty and meanness. He still remembered everything the war had done to his family and he saved his finest anger for the people who overpaid him for his work. To the Greenie, innocence was just ignorance and anyone who believed the world was a good place was criminally stupid.

But now there was a market for bitterness and the Greenie went on a rampage. The more he snarled at his customers, the more they laid out for his work. Zoltan the sculptor was big time.

I was fairly big time too. From writing book reviews for the *Varsity,* I graduated to writing a weekly column of what I liked to call "social criticism" and the CBC hired me two months before I finished university. I became a producer of tape-recorded talks between local intellectuals and the moderator of a weekly program of music, art, drama, book and movie criticism. And from that, came a regular weekly newspaper column in which I was allowed to write critically about anything that interested me. I began to develop a following.

Critics, critics, everywhere critics. Hiding under the bed, sliding down the chimneys, sneaking in the windows. A country full of critics. No great artists, no great writers, composers or choreographers but critics! Hoo boy, critics coming out of our ears. I used to think, in the days before I realized what a vain, power-hungry crew of sour old ladies the Canadian socialists really are, that if we could only get the old party to finance a little violence, we could blow up all the churches and all the banks in the country and every statue of Sir John A. Macdonald and for good measure, assassinate Pearson and Diefenbaker and Fulford and Cohen and then maybe the country would be worth living in. We would pack all the priests and ministers and rabbis and every religious nut over the age of twelve off to Africa to hand out toothbrushes to the Congolese and then maybe there would be room for the real people to move around a little.

My kind of radicalism was almost as fashionable as the Greenie's boorishness. Old Bissell had given us good advice. Be angular, let a few, but not too many, corners stick out and you'll be a man my son. I told my colleagues —God, how that pompous word used to delight me—at the CBC that I was a pacifist and I took to wearing a CND button around the office. The bomb was definitely out, even among Young Conservatives. I was very in.

"I don't understand you people," Jake said to me once. "You're all so ambitious and yet you stay here. Why don't you go to New York and really make a name for yourselves."

"Who needs New York?" I said and sank back into the upholstered rocking-chair in the upstairs bar at the Moorings. Jake's trips to Toronto had dwindled to one a year but when she showed up at Marvin's house, we all took turns taking her to the best places in town.

"You know what I think?" Jake said. "I think you're chicken. You're afraid to try your luck in the big town because you don't think you can make it there. You want to be a big fish in a small pond."

"Take another look! The pond's growing fast," I said. "Do you know that we've got more music going on here and more theatre than any other North American city outside New York? Look at the coffee houses! Look at the art galleries! Look at the boutiques! Look at the new city hall. Toronto's growing up!"

But I never doubted in my heart that I would leave Toronto someday. It was just a question of choosing the right moment to go out into the bigger world. And in the meantime, life was passing quite pleasantly. As my reputation for saying nasty things about movies, plays and books grew, my newspaper columns expanded to three a week and I began to write another column under a pseudonym for a fortnightly magazine. I bought an MG and rented a tenth-floor balcony apartment overlooking the Polka Dot Gourd coffeehouse on Avenue Road. I began to get RSVP invitations to most of the same parties the Greenie went to. We had arrived. The girls who in high school had scorned us, now sought our opinions on their art purchases, their clothes and even their sex lives. We were always happy to give them the benefit of our experience. In return, they made us adornments at their candlelit dinners. Cucumber soup, filet mignon aged, seasoned and wrapped by a caterer on Yonge Street, endive salad and cherries jubilee.

On the surface, the Greenie and I were a pair of first-class phonies. On the level below that, we were cynical and bitter about ourselves and what the people who gave us money forced us to be. How awful, we said, to have to turn into a couple of show-biz characters in order to earn a decent living. And on the level still below that, we secretly believed, so secretly we hardly ever dared let it slip into our long, sardonic conversations, that what we each were doing was basically honest and useful. On Sunday nights we had supper together, gefilte fish, cabbage borscht, onions and eggs and the Greenie's father beaming over us at the Budapest Authentic Dairy restaurant. It was the only place in Toronto where we felt completely safe.

We lost Herbie. We were so busy and he slipped away so gradually, we were hardly aware that he was gone until we got engraved invitations to his wedding. Herbert Morton Applebaum, six foot one, blond and crewcut, roaring laugh, eyes still good enough not to need glasses, captain of the Basketball Blues, Meds rep to the Students' Administrative Council, never less than third in his class, winner of the Angus Maclean Fellowship in neuro-surgery; to Enid Lucille Gardner, five foot four, Audrey Hepburn face but a little wider in the jaw and pelvis, swimming instructor at Camp Northern Pine, six years ballet, three years piano, BA in psychology and now doing a Master of

Social Work degree, at the Beth Tzedec Synagogue, Sunday, May 10, 7.30 o'clock, RSVP.

We'd never been to the Beth Tzedec before. The Greenie immediately pronounced it an authentic piece of period architecture: Miami Beach Hotel, circa 1954. Marv, as usual, tried to do the right thing. He rented a white dinner-jacket from Syd Silver. I was all right in my plain John Bullochs and Son black suit, but the Greenie, in his fawn-coloured corduroys and paisley shirt, looked like some kind of nut. We were introduced to the other guests as Herbie's oldest friends, an arm around our shoulders and a story of the times when we had lunched together every day in the high-school cafeteria. We took shelter under Herbie's patronage and felt less lonely. The three of us had been assigned as escorts for three of the bridesmaids and we sat at one of the round tables near the head table, raised on its dais.

A doctor, one of Herbie's new friends, gave the toast to the bride. And Herbie rose to reply. The caterer dimmed his lights; the movie photographer turned his up. The head table took on a rich lustre. The men in black evening dress, the women in lemon and pink gowns, their shoulders and faces, and the faces of the men, had been fattened and cleansed and oiled and rubbed with polish until they gave off a deep, almost blinding aura of well-being. This was Hollywood opening night. And we, the spectators, sitting at our tables in the darkness, our linen table-cloths littered with rich debris, scraps of smoked salmon and roast capon, stains of horseradish and spilled rye, were witnesses and allies. We at our separate tables, we were all successful barbarians; we had entered and sacked the city and now, adorned with our spoils we celebrated in luxury and ease the union of two powerful clans. All hail, long life and many children, oh yes, many, many children to

Herbert and Enid Applebaum.

Herbie thanked Enid's mother and father for bringing her up, and his own mother and father for bringing him up and his grandmother and grandfather for teaching him how to be a good Jew and Enid's grandmother and grandfather for teaching her how to keep a good Jewish home and he thanked us all for coming to help him and his new bride celebrate, especially his oldest friends. The Hollywood lights swung onto us. Marv smiled, the bridesmaids blushed and the Greenie and I tried to avoid each other's eyes. "Now join me please," Herbie's voice rose, flooded with emotion and the wonder of it all, "in a toast to my wife, I guess I can call her my wife now, my beautiful wife."

Tzena, Tzena, Tzena, Tzena,
Hab-o-noturena
Hayolim, ba-moshava

The horas came after the mambos, the cha-chas and the watusis. Our bridesmaids kicked off their satin slippers, the long candy-floss gowns slipped down from their powdered shoulders and whirled around their heavy legs. They braced their arms on our shoulders and round and round and round we went. Our circles joined other circles and soon the whole banquet room of the Beth Tzedec was going round and round. The black dinner-jackets came unbuttoned and flapped in the wind. The circle closed around Herbie and Enid and they were alone in the middle and they began to dance together, arms on each other's shoulders going round and round in the opposite direction to us. And we, turning and kicking our legs, bumping into the banks of flowers, went faster and faster, the few people still sitting down clapping and cheering us on, and we laughed and roared for Herbie to kiss the bride yet again. And he did finally when the centrifugal force broke up our circle in a tangle of caved-in chests and flying arms. Herbie stopped and deliberately, gallantly kissed his bride for what seemed like a long, long time and we all applauded and cheered. Such a beautiful wedding. May they have many, many children.

"I guess we're next, eh?" Marv said.

The waiter set two more glasses of rye and ginger ale beside us.

"You got somebody in mind?" I said.

"Not really," Marv said. "Not yet, anyway."

"What's wrong with you?" I said. I was feeling overheated from the rye and the dancing and overcome with affection for my oldest friends. No matter what they did to me downtown at the CBC, no matter how many colours they painted my coat, we were still together. We were still the boys.

"I don't understand you, Marv. You're a professional man now. You're one of the most successful young dentists in the city. You've got an office on Bloor Street and you're raking in the dough. With all that going for you, you mean to tell me you can't find a nice Jewish girl?"

"I'll make a deal with you," Marv said. "When those bridesmaids come back from the can, you pick one and I'll take the other. Six months from now, we'll make it a double ceremony."

"Watch out for the Greenie," I said. "I'll bet the bastard's got all three of them lined up already."

"That crazy Greenie," Marv said. "He hasn't changed at all, has he?"

He snagged a waiter and ordered more rye. We were alone at a soiled, moon-faced table and behind us, the wedding was breaking up. The Sammy Samuels string orchestra were tucking their violins into cases and folding up their music stands. The waiters were beginning to gather up the last plates and goblets and sweep the floor. Through the door that led into the lobby, we could see the mink coats floating toward the grand flood-lit entrance to meet the husbands and the cars. Herbie and Enid had gone, the music had stopped and the bar was closing up. No more Hollywood tonight.

"Are you still sober?" Marv said.

"More or less," I said.

"I want you to do a favour for me."

"Ask away."

"Go to Buffalo and visit Jake."

"Why should I visit Jake?"

"She's all hung up," Marv said. "I don't really know what it's all about. She won't tell me. But she's moved out of the house again and she's going crazy. She says she doesn't know anybody in Buffalo any more. She wants us all to come and see her."

"Good old Jake," I said. "The last survivor of our misspent youth."

"I keep in touch with her," Marv said. "I'm probably the only one who does. I write to her and I try to go to visit her when I can. She's a good kid, you know. I keep trying to get her to move to Toronto, but she won't. Her old man's sick and she says she won't leave Buffalo. But she says she can't stay in the same house with him any more. Crazy, eh?"

"Marvin," I said, "Marvin, we haven't seen so much of each other this last couple of years, but can I ask you a personal question?"

"Have I got into Jake Wells?"

"I wouldn't have put it so crudely."

"Funny you should ask," Marv said. "I used to think I

was the only guy in the crowd who hadn't."

The sleepy roundness of Marv's face had all been burned away. His skin was pink and taut, scrubbed bone clean in that peculiar way that dentists seem to have of being able to sterilize their flesh as well as their instruments. But dark shadows swam beneath the surface of Marv's face as in one of those lamps in which the waters of Niagara Falls appear to move because the outer glass shade is a stationary painting of the Falls while inside it a blue cylinder goes round and round creating the illusion that the river is tumbling into the gorge. When I was a child, I could never figure out how those lamps worked. And now, looking at Marv across the white linen table-cloth, I was aware of the shadows moving like banks of fog below the surface of his face but I could not see where they came from. They appeared and were gone too quickly.

"It's funny isn't it," Marv said. "I've known Jake going on ten years now. If it ever did happen, it would be almost like incest."

"Well, you could do worse things with your time than wait around for Jake," I said. "She's a good girl."

"Oh, I don't think she'll ever get married," Marv said. "And even if she did, she'd make the kind of wife who drives you back home to mother. His and Hers head-shrinkers, that sort of thing."

"Do you ever see Kathleen?"

"I used to see her once in a while," Marvin said. "Whenever she got really hung up, she'd call me and I'd take her out for supper. But she got a job in Bermuda a couple of years ago and I haven't heard from her since."

"Marvin," I said, "Marvin do you still believe in love?"

"Yes," Marvin said. "Yes, I still believe in love and in happiness too. But I've lost my spiritual cherry if that's what you mean. It happened somewhere along the way; I

68

don't even remember when. But I know, now, that I can make a mess out of my life. I used to believe there was no such thing as a bad experience. Whatever happened to me was good because it was all part of living and it would come out right in the end. Let's face it, we led pretty sheltered lives before we went to university and when I finally got there, I was hungry for action. I used to think I could do anything to myself and it wouldn't count against me. I felt I could always keep control of things, and I'd know when it was time to pull back. I thought happiness was coming to me just because I was me. I was innocent then. I know better now. I've missed it a couple of times already and who knows? If I miss it next time, that could be my last chance."

"Well, thank God there's still Jake."

"Yes," Marvin said. "There's still Jake. She's lived through much more than we have, you know. She's been hung up so often, it's almost a permanent state of mind with her now. But somehow, on her it looks good. The more she does, the more things that happen to her, the more beautiful she becomes. To me anyway. When you come right down to it, Jake really is worth waiting for."

The shadows stopped and held. They were dark pits now beneath the glossy, cared-for skin. Marvin looked like an old man, tired, gentle and haunted. He had crashed into a wall. Perhaps it was missing his year in Dents and starting life a year later than everyone else; perhaps it was Kathleen or Jake, or someone I'd never heard of. But he had crashed and fallen in a heap. Now he was waiting in the shadow of the wall, patiently gathering his strength for one last try at getting over. And his face was very beautiful.

"Well I hope you've got a few other things going for you in the meantime," I said.

"That's touching," Marvin said. "You're worried about

my sex life?"

The shadows were whirling again. Marvin's face regained its glistening opaqueness.

"I'm sorry," I said. "I tend to get pompous late at night. It's an occupational hazard for people who work at the CBC."

"I do all right," Marvin said. "If you wanted to see me in the office, you'd have to wait six weeks for an appointment. I could be a rich man if I wanted to give up my evenings and weekends. As it is, I make enough to live and I still have money left over to play around on the market with. I live at home but I keep an apartment downtown too. I have a Pontiac convertible and I can get laid just about whenever I feel in the mood for it. I'm leading a pretty good life."

"We're getting old," I said. "Getting laid now is almost too easy."

"We're getting what we wanted," Marvin said.

"You know, Marvin, we should see each other more. We mustn't get too wrapped up in business."

"You're right," Marv said. "Old friends are still the best friends."

That was almost the last time I ever saw Marvin.

Partly out of curiosity, partly because of Marv, and partly because I was 27 and it was the first night warm enough to drive with the top of my MG down, I went to Buffalo one Friday night a couple of weeks later to see Jake. The whole city seemed to be moving with me, our headlights making a fluid trail through the trumpeting signs of the neon encampment on the edge of Toronto. Then the long, straight, hurrying stretch to Hamilton, the hot blue sky filled with lights; airplanes, stars, road lamps and huge neon symbols at Oakville, "Ford" and "GE," pop art blazing out over the fruit trees. Crossing the Burlington Skyway, the red steeple of flame over the Hamilton steelworks on my right, the open water of the bay on my left, as vast and dark as an ocean and singing "My Funny Valentine" along with Ella Fitzgerald on the stereophonic tape-recorder in my car, I felt I could drive on forever.

Jake took me first to a coffee house because she wanted me to see her first big affair. It had been all over for almost five years now, she explained, but they were still good friends. Jake was as nervous and confused as Marv had said. But he was right too, that her troubles had taken nothing from her. You looked at her, you knew she had been with men and that there was no position unknown to her now. Wrinkles had been added to the eyes of the Chinese doll smile. The eyes took in everything, watching and waiting quietly. They were no longer capable of registering be-musement, only amusement. Jake had seen it all before. Yet I knew too, watching her through the sweetish, dark smoke of the coffee house that Jake had become even more vulnerable. She was even hungrier for the good things of life. Her lacquered hair and delicate make up, her smart pink linen suit and Victorian gold earrings, were what she had learned to wear to catch the attention of men. Every-thing about her said she had had enough of boys. Next time around, she wanted the real thing.

I told her about my work at the CBC. She told me about how she was decorating her new apartment; the art lessons she was still taking, this time privately with a painter named Bruno who had just had a one-man show in Newark, and how glad she was to see such an old friend. It had been so long, she said, since she had had someone she could really talk to.

Jake's first lover came to our table. They had a little chat about the Bergman festival that was on in town and the lover, whose name was Bill, steered clear of me. Jake introduced me as a leading Toronto critic and Bill seemed to melt in my direction waiting to be approved and patted.

I could see why Jake had been an easy mark for him. He was one of three partners in the coffee house; she had worked there for a couple of months as a waitress. He was from Minnesota and had two years at Harvard and three in the army. Two of his army years he'd done in Germany and he was full of funny stories about those lovable old Europeans. He talked about LSD and pot and peyote as though he'd invented them.

From what Jake had told me, he'd got her just when she was moving out of her father's house the first time and going through a very bad period. A hospital psychologist was giving her two free hours a week to help her decide what she meant when she said, "I want to be independent." She'd been ready to listen to almost anyone who sounded reasonably happy. Bill was very American and very self assured. He had the charm of the career drifter, that ability to concentrate all his abilities on whatever activity engaged him at the moment. He was tall and so casual he seemed to have spent hours just making himself up. Khaki chinos, a blue button-down shirt with no tie, a crew cut with every stunted hair in place, knife thin, evenly tanned face, and small, pointed ears. His voice was surprisingly deep and melodious. He could turn it on you like a hose. Jake had asked her psychologist what to do and he had told her she was old enough to start making her own decisions. So she went off to her friendly old neighbourhood family doctor and he wrote her a prescription for the pill and she was off and running. It had been fine for six months until what Jake chose to call an "older woman, if you know what I mean," had scooped up her Bill and run away with him.

"He's a sweet boy, he really is," Jake said later when we were alone in her apartment. "Now that everything's over,

I mean now that he's deflowered me and all that, I can see him as he actually is. I'm discovering that I can like him now just as a person."

"I think he's a prick," I said. Her whole apartment and the arrangements she had made for how we were to spend the night had irritated me and I wanted to strike back. I was angry at the way she seemed to think she could assign me a role too and that I would just docilely slip into it. I wanted to tell her about all the women in Toronto who would have been delighted to have me sitting in their bedrooms.

"You don't understand," she said. "Going to see him is a kind of therapy for me. It makes me realize how far I've come since then. Besides, he's very mixed up and he needs a friend. I make a very good friend, you know."

"So do I," I said. "But don't trust me. None of my other friends do."

"Oh stuff your tough-guy act," Jake said. "I've known you too long."

She swished out to the kitchen to get me another can of Budweiser. Her legs below the short nightgown and robe were surprisingly thin and white. Without her make-up and restraining underwear, Jake was so soft and warm and desirable that I was finding it an effort of will to keep from reaching out and grabbing her.

Jake had already given me notice that any advances would definitely not be welcome. She was going to sleep on the couch and I was to have the bed. The couch was an early American relic curved up at both ends and the only way anyone could possibly sleep on it was to curl up into a foetal ball. The apartment was the top floor of a rundown old house and Jake had embellished it with antiques. There was a rosewood commode, a schoolteacher's writing-desk, a big round wooden table, the couch and a big, old-fashioned four-poster bed. Jake had prowled the junk shops and furnished the place for less than $200. She had stripped all the paint and varnish off the wood herself and refinished it with linseed oil. She'd painted the walls stark white but she'd softened the effect by hanging prints and pictures that she'd clipped from magazines and pasted onto cardboard to make collages. And too, she'd scattered bright orange and brown cushions around the floor. But her prize possession was a photograph of an old cavalry-man that she'd bought in a second-hand bookstore for 50 cents and had framed. He looked like a Hungarian Hussar or something, all decked out in a shako, sword and sash filled with medals, and glowering sternly in front of the photographer's black drapes. What made the picture so good was the fact that the Hussar was completely cross-eyed.

No interior decorator, no hot-shit hot shot from *McCall's* or *Esquire* or even *Playboy* could have put together anything half so lovely as Jake's apartment. Jake had no money; the place smelled of frugality. The furniture was old and there wasn't much of it. Yet under Jake's hand, the barrenness became airiness; the apartment was free and clean. The mellow glow from the linseed-oiled furniture gave off an air of deep warmth, as though a fire were burning somewhere in the apartment in a hidden grate. The scattered pillows and posters of bullfights, old Sears-Roebuck ads for liniment and long johns, *art nouveau* ladies in sweeping hats all proclaimed Jake's whimsy and perfect taste. The crowning touch was the photograph of the cross-eyed Hussar. He stared out over the rooms in mute and hilarious disapproval. He was Jake's ironic comment on everything she had done with the apartment.

The gaiety that Jake had constructed around her was all the finer and more moving because it was balanced precariously on the edge of an abyss. There had been other lovers after Bill. Everything from one-night stands to a year-long, off-and-on affair with a married man. The psychologist had snapped her out of it. He'd called her a tramp. He was a nasty, sarcastic little man, Jake said, but he was helping her to understand certain things about her own life. She saw clearly now, she said, that she had been using sex to avoid facing up to other problems. Now she could take men or leave them alone. Mostly, she preferred to leave them alone. She didn't want any kind of attachment now; not until she had worked out her life a little better. She said this facing me, her legs curled up under her on the bed, while I was stretched out on the couch watching her. I chose to ignore her warnings. I wanted her desperately. She had a new job, she went on. Girl Friday in an art gallery. She pretty well ran the place, selling pictures, arranging shows, fussing over the artists and doing the books while the owner sat in the back room pouring Kaopectate over his ulcer. That's how she met Bruno. He was the most talented painter, she said, on the gallery's list. They got on together. She cooked the occasional meal for him. He gave her lessons and criticized her work. Another warning. Her eyes turned empty and cold watching me.

I snarled and then I pouted. I certainly hadn't come all the way to Buffalo just for that, I said. What did she take me for? And after all the years she had known me! Just to prove the point, I insisted that she should have the bed and I was going to sleep on the malformed couch. No, definitely not, Jake insisted. She couldn't allow it. After all, I was still her guest. We argued into the night and finally, I suggested a compromise. We could divide the bed in half. Jake was wary, but I swore I was interested only in a good night's sleep for both of us. At last, Jake gave in. She was too tired to fight any more.

75

She lay down on her side and stared resolutely at the wall. I lay down beside her and stared rigidly at the ceiling. I was too inflamed with lust and anger to sleep but within a few minutes, I heard Jake snoring softly beside me. I lay rigid, staring straight up. In the darkness, the shadows on the ceiling were the colour of mouse fur. I was afraid to move, afraid even to twitch, lest I lose all self-control, and throw myself on top of Jake. Patience, I counselled myself. Patience, there is still one more night to spend in this room with her. The time wasn't ripe yet. I felt I had entered a new and dangerous world when I had swung my MG out onto the Peace Bridge between Fort Erie and Buffalo. The bridge rose out of the dark, somnolent fields of the Niagara Peninsula, and then descended sharply. Sliding down into the smoke and flaming red neon signs of Buffalo, I had left the known world behind me. I was alone and unarmed with Jake. I had only my nerve and guile with which to win her. And Marvin had been right all along. Jake was worth waiting for.

The next day was filled with sun and the smell of new grass. We went to watch a balloon ascension. It was being staged by the Knox-Albright Gallery for a show of something called "Three Centuries of Niagara Falls." Jake, for all her tough talk about art, wasn't interested at all in the paintings. But she was mad to see the balloon go up. I spread my trench coat on the spongy ground of Delaware Park and we watched the crew in their white coveralls fussing over the burners and the balloon. The burners looked like huge camp stoves. They heated the air and other bits of machinery, fans and pipes, pumped it into the balloon. The balloon was still only a round white sheet lying on the ground with a wickerwork basket tied to it. Ropes led from the balloon to a ring of cars. The cars would anchor it until it was ready to float up and over the Falls.

I felt uneasy. This park was strange ground to me; these were strange people. Their faces were more vivid than the faces of Canadians and their clothes were more stylish. The men wore narrow black and grey slacks pressed as sharp as knife blades and narrowly striped black and crimson shirts, with tiny, button-down collars open at the neck. The women wore tartan Bermuda shorts and sack dresses and A shapes in solid colours, blue, orange and green. The women were as bright and hard as diamonds. I thought what a Saturday afternoon in a Toronto park would be like. The men would be in grey flannels and tweed jackets or blue blazers. The women would be wearing pleated white skirts and pastel blouses. And the faces of the Canadians would be fuller and rougher. Then too, if someone were sending a balloon aloft from a Toronto park, the park would be jammed. It would be an occasion and some civic big shot would be there to make a speech while the flashbulbs popped and the boys from the dailies scribbled notes. But in Buffalo, only a handful, maybe 30 people in all, had come out to watch the balloon go up. There was so much going on around them; they had so many ways in which to pass their time. The launching of the balloon was just a tick mark in the weekend round of events scheduled to enlighten and amuse them. They watched the bustle of preparations silently. Their faces were smooth and lean, and their eyes were cool. Their eyes were wise. They seemed to have seen and known so much more than I had. I am just like them, I thought. And they are not like me at all.

"Max," Jake said. "Can I ask you a personal question? Are you happy, Max?"

"I'm contented," I said. "I'm a man of limited ambition."

"I thought you would have gone to New York a long time ago."

"Maybe I should have gone. But it's too late now."

"You talk like an old man," Jake said.

"I have more power than some men twice my age," I said. "I have an office with a rug on the floor and my own secretary. When I have something to say, people listen to me. And they pay me, they pay me very well indeed, for talking. I'm in a funny kind of business. If you're bright and you hustle and you get the breaks, you can move up very fast. And I'm way ahead right now of all the people I started out with. I can't see myself giving all that up to start over again somewhere else."

"But you're still in Toronto," Jake said. "You used to be very bitter about Toronto."

The balloon began to inflate. It became a huge white onion and the wind tore at it. The crew fought a grim battle with the anchor ropes to keep it from blowing away before its time. A couple dressed in Gay Nineties costumes appeared and waited to climb into the wickerwork gondola. The man wore white ducks, an embroidered riverboat gambler's vest, a red-and-white striped blazer and a straw boater. The woman wore a high-necked green gown and a green bonnet. The wind lifted the gown, revealing that she'd even taken the trouble to put on a silly-looking pair of ankle-length white bloomers. I snickered, but nobody else in the crowd made a sound. I had the feeling that these Americans could have been watching an atom bomb go off and they would have remained just as cool and detached.

"Toronto has changed," I said. "It has all the trappings of a big city now; homosexual bars, half a dozen good restaurants, Go Go dancers, subways, LSD, the Mafia. What more could anyone ask for?"

"And you're a big shot there," Jake said. "That's a little hard for me to get used to."

"I've carved a niche," I said. "I'm ready to tell the rest of the country to go to hell. Lester Pearson looks and talks like Porky Pig and the slobs who might replace him are even more greedy and boring. The Americans already own more of the country than we do and the French are working themselves up to such a fever pitch of self-pity that they may finally blow the whole damned thing into little pieces. Canada's a hell of a place if you stop and think about it too much. So I'm teaching myself not to think about it."

"And yet you stay there," Jake said. "You're getting mellow in your old age."

" 'Tis a poor thing, but mine own'" I said.

The balloon was almost full and the wind bashed at it. The crews holding the anchor ropes fought to hold it down until the Gay Nineties couple at least climbed into the gondola, but the wind was so powerful it stretched the ropes taut and lifted some of the crew off the ground. Their legs flapped wildly in the air; they looked like insects trying to hold back the surge of a giant tulip with strands of spider web. Finally, one crew lost control completely. The rope slithered away from them and cracked like a whip. The balloon seemed to rest delicately against a lamppost and then it sank to the ground. The jutting street lamp had torn the fabric. The balloon collapsed into a crinkled white sheet again. The Gay Nineties man fished a cigar out from somewhere in the mysteries of his outfit and lit it on the flames of one of the hot-air machines. The crowd watched the disaster impassively and then began to drift away.

"That's Buffalo for you," Jake said. "They can't even blow up a balloon without fucking it up."

On the way home, we went shopping at the A & P and while Jake went back to her apartment to cook the chicken, I went on to the liquor store. It was like entering a crystal wonderland. In those days, the Liquor Control Board of Ontario still kept all its bottles hidden in bins. You could never be sure of what you'd bought until the clerk was actually wrapping it for you. An American liquor store appeared, by contrast, like a magic cornucopia. There were bottles everywhere. They stood in orderly rows on the floor; they rose to the ceiling, in shelves and racks; they were piled with mad abandon on three waist-high tables in the centre of the room, they hung like magazines from half a dozen twirling racks. There were strange names from distant and romantic places, Kahlua, Aquavit, Retsina, Slivovitz, Fundador, Liebfraumilch, La Creme a Christi, Saki, and names I had learned from magazine ads: Jack Daniels, Cutty Sark, Drambuie, Beefeater, Irish Mist, Mumm's Cordon Rouge and even Canadian Club. There was French wine in dusty-looking bottles, and American wine in everything from six splits in a carton to gallon jugs. And there was every kind of beer from Lowenbrau and Bass Ale to Utica Club. The dream of the rich fast life, the apartment in San Francisco, Bobby Kennedy, Jean Shrimpton, Carnaby Street and the Playboy Clubs, it had all been poured into bottles and mass distributed. All the liquid pleasure of the world, more variety than Roman emperors, French kings or English merchant princes had ever been able to command was waiting for Americans at their neighbourhood liquor store. For a long time, I stood motionless in the midst of this sparkling treasure, a dazzled hick from the true north, strong and free. I finally settled on a bottle of Gordon's gin, two bottles of Prince de Galles sauterne and a bottle of Courvoisier. Climbing the steps back to Jake's apartment, the bottles clunking seductively in their brown paper bag, I told myself tonight could be the night. Maybe Jake, like me, is beginning to wonder about what she had been missing all these years. I had a sense of historic occasion.

We ate dinner by the light of two candles set in wooden holders that Jake had found during her sweeps through the local junk stores. The candle-holders had been carved and painted to look like two circus clowns. By the time we had finished the chicory salad and the Danish blue cheese, Jake was drunk and I was feeling no pain. We had our chocolate-chip-peppermint-stick ice cream sitting on the floor under the picture of the cross-eyed Hussar. We drank a full percolator of strong black coffee and killed almost a third of the brandy. I half-led, half-carried Jake to the bed.

My fingers were trembling as I undressed her. Each time I removed a garment, I paused to soothe and still her flutterings. Her tongue filled my mouth. My fingers traced patterns on her soft, full breasts. The wet wool smell, powerful and amorous, rose in waves from Jake and filled the room.

But she stiffened when I tried to take her panties off. My thumb remained inside the elastic. Her hand clamped over mine. Her eyes remained closed. Haste makes waste, I told myself. Gently, gently, gently. Besides, it was almost an academic question. Jake had graduated from sensible white cotton underwear to sheer black bikini panties. No sense in making a fuss about them, I decided. They would slip away, disappear in a puff of smoke, soon enough.

We fondled each other. We rolled back and forth on the bed. Jake bit my neck and unbuttoned my shirt. She pressed herself to my chest. But her silly little panties remained firmly, insultingly in place. Each time I tried to slip them down she stopped me. I grew furious at her and finally, when I had her hands busy elsewhere, I reached down and yanked her panties off. Jake sprang back from me as though her arms were steel springs.

"What's wrong with you?" she said.

81

"We've already done this bit," I said. "We used to play this game when we were kids. We're not kids any more."

"Then don't throw a temper tantrum because you can't have a lollipop," Jake said.

She looked suddenly old and haggard and quite capable of slitting my throat. I sat and lit a cigarette. Jake flounced to the closet, wrapped a heavy terrycloth bathrobe around herself and came back to sit on the bed. She was cold sober.

"I'm sorry," she said. "Please, Max, don't be angry with me."

"Don't be silly," I said. "Of course I'm not angry. Why should I be angry? But I must admit I am curious."

"I have to be very selfish now," Jake said. "I'm trying to work through a lot of my own problems, and I have to concentrate like hell on them. I can't afford to give myself to anyone."

"What about Bruno? He doesn't sound like the type who comes for free."

"Bruno doesn't count," Jake said. "He's a narcissistic little son of a bitch. It doesn't mean anything to him so it doesn't mean anything to me either. I'm safe with Bruno."

"You seem to think you're safe with the whole world," I said. "But don't count on it. Some of us aren't as dumb as Bruno or as patient as Marvin."

"Don't be nasty," Jake said. "I'm trying to be completely honest with you. Marv's the kind of person I could eventually marry. But if I let him sleep with me—or if I let you sleep with me, for that matter—I'd lose you both as friends. And right now, I need friends a lot more than I need lovers. If I got started with Marvin now, it would have to end in a big hangup because neither one of us is ready for anything like a permanent commitment. But if we hang on for a while, keep cool, maybe we'll make it yet."

"What are you after, Jake? What the hell do you really want?"

"In 25 words or less? I want to be happy."

"Bah! Humbug!" I said. "Happiness is the opiate of the middle class."

"Oh come off it, Max. You're not young enough to be that cynical. Happiness is only a compromise anyway. It's a no-man's-land between what you want to do and what other people tell you you have to do. That's what I'm working on now. I'm trying to sort out the things that aren't really important and push them out of my life. And that can be pretty painful. But it's something I have to do. I'm trying to find out who I am before it's too late."

"What you're doing is a losing proposition," I said. "By the time you find yourself, you're already lost again. You've changed during the time you were looking. And then you have to start all over again looking for this new person you've turned into. Trying to find yourself is the ultimate self-delusion. It's perpetual masturbation."

"Maybe it is, Max. Maybe you're right. But it's all I've got and I'm sticking to it. I don't want to be a 30-year-old neurotic."

"What if you find yourself and wake up to discover that you've lost the world?" I said. "You call it independence but the real word for it is individualism. Me! Me! Me! You refuse point blank to take any responsibility for what's going on around you. There's a war in Vietnam and there's going to be a war in South America. Africa's on the verge of anarchy and India's on the edge of revolution. The sky's turning black over you and the Negroes are rising under you and every day, in some city in the world, there's a riot of some kind and people are getting shot down in the streets. And all you can worry about is whether you're going to grow up happy. People like you are the curse of western civilization."

"What are you doing about the world, Max?"

"At the moment? Not very much. But I worry a lot."

"I'm sure that's a great comfort to the boys in Vietnam."

"All I could do in Vietnam is get killed," I said. "It's not my country and it's not my war. I don't understand enough about it to be of use to anyone there. But when the good fight comes to Canada, I will be able to do something. I know the people I live with and I can talk their language. And I'm close enough to the action in Canada that I'm beginning to learn where the levers are and how to pull them to make the machine go. The problems are universal: overpopulation, the arms race, automation, drugs—God I could go on for hours. I'm the world's champion magazine reader and I know every, quote, significant problem, unquote, that's come down the pipe in the last ten years. But it all boils down to one thing: people with open minds, people who are ready for change, against people with closed minds, the ones who want to keep the world the way it's always been. The people who want to live against the people who are already dead. In Canada, things are still static. The dead people are still running the show. But the country's going to wake up soon. And when it does, I'll be there and I'll be able to do something. If I go to Vietnam, or anywhere else for that matter, I'm just a tourist."

"You talk big Max. But what if it never comes to Canada? What if Canada stays a 'backwater of western civilization,' like you always used to call it?"

"It'll come," I said. "It's rising up from Washington and it's spreading all over the world. It's like bubonic plague. Every time Johnson opens his mouth, he throws up more germs."

"But what if you're wrong," Jake said. "You sound so

sure of yourself, but what if you spend all your life in Toronto waiting for something to happen there and it never does?"

"It'll come," I said. "I know it will. I just know it will."

"You're right," Jake said. "Of course you're right. You're always right."

She came forward on the bed and kissed me on the lips, a gentle, tender, almost motherly kiss. We fell back together on the rumpled sheets and we kissed and explored each other. I tried to make love to her again and again and again. I was mad with desire. I had to have Jake now; I had to own her outright. But Jake gently but firmly rebuffed me. She allowed herself to take and to give a careful, almost dainty pleasure but she always drew back. At last she fell asleep, her head resting on my shoulder and her hand resting, in a soft, uncommitted way on my crotch.

The night was over. Weak rays of sunlight, like a straw broom, pushed the darkness back from Jake's room. I contemplated rolling Jake over and raping her. But I was afraid. I wanted her too much to risk anything that would lose her for me now. My head was stuffed with broken glass. I went over in my mind each instant of the night, trying to figure out where I had failed to push my luck or where I had pushed it too hard. I lay still, sucking the last bits of sleep from the dry air.

The next day, I had to leave early. I had a program to prepare and tape at four in the afternoon and a magazine column to write. We had breakfast on the small sunporch that adjoined Jake's kitchen. She cooked scrambled eggs and green onions and mixed the gin with frozen orange juice. We ate and drank under a flag of truce. When the time came for me to go, Jake walked with me to the car. She hugged me and kissed me on the lips and said she wanted to see me again as soon as possible.

I drove back to Toronto through the baking, oppressive afternoon. I was overcome by a sense of irrecoverable loss. I could break into tears, I could break into a thousand painful little pieces. So much time I had let slip through my fingers. Perhaps it was already too late; perhaps I had already lost Jake somewhere along the way. Jake had met and defeated me in the last two nights. We had come so close and yet we were still ununited. Jake was still scratching at her problems alone and I was still lonely. Yet there is still time, I told myself. Not a lot of time, but time.

I rolled past Prud'homme's Garden Centre, its neon lights shining weakly, obscenely, in the shadowless glare. I saw that everything we had done, the four of us, the boys in Toronto, had been, unconsciously at least, a race to catch up to Jake Wells. And without intending to, without even knowing that we were after her, she had stayed ahead of us. We had set out to make our way in the world and we had prospered. We had learned to be supple; our cleverness had grown into shrewdness. We were almost wise. And yet Jake, in her scatterbrained way, could still perform with greater assurance and style than we could muster; she could still lead her life with greater intensity than we could hope to attain. Jake never sought the knowledge that put her always beyond us. She didn't have to seek it. That knowledge was all around her. It invaded her by osmosis. It overwhelmed her. Jake was part of the big show and we were part of the little show and nothing could ever change that.

Still, I told myself, one shouldn't bite the tradition that pays the bills. Being part of the little show was the reason I could make a good living as a kind of freelance critic. I was an end product of Canadian history. Canadians had spent so much time watching the big show that they had developed a good eye for it. They were affected by what happened in the big show but there wasn't one damned thing they could do about changing anything that happened there. So they watched in a helpless, raging frustration and they learned to pick out every weak spot, every tiny flaw in the facade of the big show. It was our national indoor sport. And I was only a small refinement, just enough to make my voice worth listening to from time to time, on what everyone in Canada had been doing since childhood.

I drove on through fields bleached to the colour of dull steel by the searing heat. Outside Hamilton, the Queen E began the slow descent into the curve that would launch it toward Toronto. It was like a catapult that would hurl me back to the city and my own importance. The curve swept out and out, beyond all signs of human life, a thin black line through the southern Ontario tundra, and it was carrying me away from the beauty and the drama of the world that Jake Wells lived in.

I had been cheated. I cursed myself for a mark and a blind, stupid fool. I had been seduced by the dream of Toronto and now I was about to pay for my gullibility. In the years when I was coming of age, Toronto had been turning into a big city. Toronto and I had grown up together. And now the city was filled with noise and activity and some of what the artists and actors and musicians were doing there was as good as anyone anywhere in the world. I believed that with all my heart.

But Toronto was not a world capital. And this knowledge tormented me. The people who lived on ideas in London and New York and San Francisco and maybe even still Paris, counted for something in history because their audience was bigger and the people who listened to them were the people who made the decisions that mattered in the world. And the people who did the same things in

Toronto might even be better at it, but they counted for little because the people who paid attention to them had no real decisions at all to make.

I tried to draw some comfort from the past. After all, I told myself, when Grieg and Ibsen were working in Oslo, and Kierkegaard was suffering in Copenhagen and when Faulkner was writing in Oxford, Mississippi, these were hardly important cities in the world. But what good did such comparisons do? Those men had possessed the genius to lift themselves from obscurity. And I was not a genius or anything even close to it.

But why should I care in the end whether my city was important or not? There was still enough going on there that I could lead a full and interesting life in Toronto. But the good life, I realized bitterly, was just not good enough for me. I still wanted to feel I was in, or at least near, the centre of things. If you do not believe in an afterlife, then you have to believe that your life here is important, that you have at least the chance of being remembered, the chance for glory.

Toronto rushed out to meet me. The flat, suburban factories with the glass brick walls lined both sides of the highway. Behind them, the squat bungalows, looking like dolls' houses with their shoulder-high trees and parched, weedy lawns marched along curlicued suburban streets southward to the lake and northward to Highway 401 and beyond it. I roared past the high, bleak, Tip Top Tailors factory and Loblaws Warehouse and turned off the lakefront at York Street, coming out of the cool tunnel to the mountainous, soot-covered Royal York Hotel and the hot, silent emptiness of the downtown Toronto streets on a Sunday afternoon.

It's not so bad, I told myself. There are a lot worse places in the world than this. There are advantages to belonging to the little show. We are more stable here. We are not destroyed by every new variety of emotion. We may be duller than the Americans but we are more self-reliant. We are cooler. We are a country stitched together with compromises and we have learned how to be calm and rational. I tried to impart some of this sense of stability in my letters to Jake. I believed I was in love with her. But any display of passion might frighten her off, I thought, while a gentle and understanding friend could well grow into a lover. Her replies grew longer and more involved, page after page scrawled in green ink. She urged and then begged me to come to Buffalo. I kept trying to get a few columns ahead and plan around my program schedule so that I could get away but it was a busy time. Finally, Jake came to Toronto but I didn't see her even then. And as things worked out, I never saw her again.

She came to Toronto on a Tuesday afternoon. It was a sudden impulse. She had to see me, she said, and she called me from the bus station. I told her to take a cab to the Park Plaza and wait for me there. I had a full schedule of programs and meetings that were supposed to keep me inside the radio building until seven that night, but I told Jake I would get somebody to take over for me. I tore around desperately looking for someone to fill my place. The musty green corridors of the radio building, all the people padding through the halls, the girls, busy and gabbing over their typewriters, all seemed a conspiracy to keep me from Jake. This time, I was sure, something would happen for us. She would stay at my place and my apartment had only one bed, no couches. Our letters had already laid the groundwork. Not for marriage maybe, marriage was still a big word, but certainly for something solider than mere friendship. I would replace Marvin; I would become Jake's secret insurance policy. And when she was ready, she would come to me. She would commit herself to me. But there was no-one to take over my programs. All the other producers in my department had jobs of their own to do. They were sympathetic, they commiserated with me, but they couldn't, they said, help it if they were all tied up. And at five o'clock my supervisor caught me running toward the stairs, caught my arm as he would have hooked and netted a terrified fish and pulled me into his office. The big meeting was about to begin. A big new program was being planned for Thursday nights, three solid hours of Kultur. I was to be one of four producers sharing responsibility for it. What did I think of this, that and the other thing? I thought only a masochist would listen to three solid hours of such pretentiousness. All I could really think about was Jake. And all the apple cheeks and green tweed gathered around my supervisor's desk were keeping me from her. But I didn't get up and stalk from the room. I didn't even excuse myself long enough to call Jake at the bar. A job is a job. At the CBC, you go up or you die. They were offering me a free hand with my quarter of the programs. I could do almost anything I wanted with them as long as I cleared it first with my supervisor. The opportunity was too good to miss. I added my pipe smoke to the general fog in the room. I smiled modestly and joked politely and I stated my ideas vaguely enough to leave myself plenty of room for manoeuvring.

By the time I got to the roof of the Park Plaza, Jake was gone. My waiter, John, remembered her. She had sat alone all afternoon and when the five o'clock crowd began to fill up the bar, she had left. No message. I tried to get drunk but I had lost the knack, even for that. I went out to the terrace and leaned over the balustrade and thought idly of jumping off it, knowing all the while I was too great a coward for that too.

I came as close that night as I have ever been able to manage to actually hating myself. I knew perfectly well that I could easily have left the planning meeting at the CBC to telephone Jake. My colleagues would not have been at all offended. They might even have applauded my little handclap of independence. See, he does have a private life! Look, he isn't a slave to his career at the CBC. He risks offending people once in a while. Taking time out to call Jake might well have won me a few points at the CBC.

Instead, I had used my work as an excuse. Work was a drug. As long as I could say I had work to do, I didn't have to think too much. The thing just ahead, the job to be done, was all that mattered. I had already reached the plateau where I hardly noticed the money and I wasn't even particularly interested in power any more. I already had more power than I knew what to do with. Even the fame, the strangers coming up to say how they had been amused or outraged by something I had written or said on television, was becoming irrelevant. I knew too much about the ugly mechanics of being a known person to be much impressed by attention from people outside the business. Still I kept at it, working twelve and fourteen hours a day and treating the weekend as only another couple of days to get things done. I worked hard because working hard was all I really knew how to do.

None of this had ever impressed Jake very much. She lived in a world far beyond the dour, southern Ontario ethic that work maketh the good man. For Jake, there was no justification through hard work alone. She wanted people to come to her naked and afraid. With Jake, you were honest or you were not worth bothering about. I was not prepared to leave behind all I was doing and just be. I wouldn't have known how to just be even if I had wanted to try it. Perhaps I was afraid of Jake. Perhaps I was a victim of my own acute self-knowledge. Perhaps I was just not capable of loving someone the way Jake demanded love. I don't know. All I know is that when the chance came to have Jake all to myself, I ran away from it.

Looking south from the Plaza roof I could see the high office buildings with the windows here and there still lit. Cleaning women, I supposed, going about the lonely business of clearing away the day's debris to make room for the manufacture of tomorrow's debris. And looking east and west, I could see the traffic winding through the coloured lights of Bloor Street, a million people all busy enjoying the summer night. Good old Toronto.

About a year later, I got my last letter from Jake. It was really just a note on the back of a card. The card said:

Doctor and Mrs. Norton Welinsky
Are Pleased to Announce the Marriage of Their Daughter,
Jacqueline Anne,
to
Capt. Michael Abrams, USMC,
the Son of Mr. and Mrs. Louis Abrams

On the back, Jake had written, "Dearest Max, sorry you didn't get to kiss the bride. Very small ceremony. Just us and two witnesses. On our way now to Florida. Mickey's stationed at Pensacola. If you ever get down that way, be sure to look us up. Meantime, take care of yourself and do great things. You're still one of my favourite people, you know. Lots of hugs, Jake."

We'd known that Jake was getting married. Marv had taken a trip to Buffalo and found her already engaged and shopping for her trousseau. But I still couldn't believe she had finally settled on a Marine officer. It just didn't seem possible that Jake was going to live the rest of her life with a military man. Captain Michael Abrams! What kind of life could she possibly have with him? Why in God's name had she done it?

"What you think?" the Greenie said. "She should want to spend the rest of her life with bums like us?"

"But a Marine!" I said. "She could have got herself something better than that!"

"American army's good pay," the Greenie said. "Officer's a big deal. American army they give you a medal every time you wipe your ass."

"He's not a soldier, goddamn it. He's a Marine."

"Same kind difference," the Greenie said, and shovelled more cabbage borscht into his mouth.

For a long time, I had been too busy for our weekly dinners but now I was starting to get on top of things again and I'd taken to meeting the Greenie on Sunday nights at the Budapest Authentic Dairy restaurant.

"She should have waited for one of us," I said. "We could have done so much for her."

"Marry Jake? You're thinking crazy," the Greenie said. "Such a mixed-up little broad."

"Well, I wish I'd slept with her," I said. "I guess that's what I really regret. It would have given me something to remember."

"Jake was a lousy lay."

"How the hell would you know?"

"How you think?"

"You're lying through your teeth!"

"Why I have to lie?" the Greenie said. He was in a jovial mood. Jake's marriage had amused him greatly. "You think I don't get enough women any time I want them? You think I have to make up stories? Listen to me, schmock! Remember that big day you send Jake to a bar to

93

wait for you all afternoon and you never show up? She calls me. Big deal, she has to talk to someone. Some guy in Buffalo is giving her a hard time. She comes around to my studio and I listen to her. What the hell else I got to do in the afternoons? And pretty soon, one thing leads to another. She's all hung-up; she thinks she's not a real woman anymore. Some bullshit like that. So I help her find out. For that day, I'm the Salvation Army."

"You lying bastard!" I said.

"One hand on tit, the other hand on ass, squeeze, she opens up and in I go."

"Now I know you're lying," I said.

"You don't know nothing about women," the Greenie said. "I'm starting to worry about you. You should come around to see me more. I give you good advice. What the hell? Maybe I even find something for you to practise on. Now listen to me, schmock! Jake is not a whore, right? Right! Now the next lesson: she likes it. Every broad likes it. And for a little while in their lives, they'll take it anywhere they can get it, right? Right! So it just happens when Jake comes to see me that day, she is in one of those moods. She wants it and I just happen to be there. If you're there, you get it. If Marv's there, maybe she even goes down for him. Same thing with getting married. Like an animal, an instinct. She wants security, a house, a car, all the bullshit. Only she never admits it. All her life she's kidding herself. Then one day, she looks in the mirror; she sees she's already not looking so good. The next guy that comes along, he's it. Just like that. Bang, bang, bang!"

It took me a long time to realize that Jake had finally left us. We had all been wrong about her. She didn't put up much of a fight after all. It seemed as though the first time she had been really scared, she had run. Or perhaps it was only that she had moved on into a world where we would never be able to follow her. Perhaps her new life was fuller and more intense that anything we could ever hope for. I wondered if Mickey Abrams would be sent to Vietnam and what Jake would do then.

We all felt we'd lost something but Marv lost even more than we did. He'd gone to Buffalo to see her and found that she'd given up the apartment and was already too occupied with her new life to bother with him. She had only a few minutes to spare for him and then she was gone. He wrote me about it from Buffalo.

"Dear Max," his letter said: "I've just come from having breakfast with Jake. You'll see by this stationery that I'm staying at the good old Statler Hotel. Jake's back with her family. She's getting married in a couple of days to an army captain or something. She was pretty vague about what he does for a living. She told me to tell you she's going to write you a long letter explaining it all, but she hasn't had time to so far because everything was so sudden. She just barely had time to have breakfast with me this morning because she's running all over the city buying things. She insisted we go to this seafood place and have a dozen clams each. Clams are her new kick. Right now, I'm not feeling so good. Raw clams and beer are not exactly my idea of a good hearty breakfast.

"Anyway, that's not why I'm writing. I've decided to take my vacation right now instead of in September like I'd planned. I'm feeling kind of tired and depressed and I need some time off. I want to ask a favour of you, old cock. Would you just go down to my office and sort of keep an eye on things a couple of times this week? I know you're busy, but I'd really appreciate it. I've written my nurse, Mrs. Butcher, to stall my appointments for a week and I don't have anything in the book that's very urgent. Mrs. Butcher's pretty good and I think she can handle my patients, but I'd like you to just sort of drop in and see how she's doing. Thanks again, Marv."

I did as Marv asked. I went over to his office three times that week but there wasn't anything for me to do. Mrs. Butcher turned out to be a grey-haired, motherly woman and she had everything well in hand. She told all his patients that Marv had a bad case of flu and made appointments for them later in the month. She spent her own time scrubbing the floors and walls and answering the telephone. I felt sorry for her. There is something inhuman about a dentist's office when the dentist isn't there. The drills look like mechanical monsters.

Marv never did come back. We heard rumours that he was in Mississippi working for civil rights, that he was living in the Village on pot and LSD; that he'd joined the Navy and was fixing teeth on a carrier off Vietnam and that he'd gone to Israel and was living on a kibbutz. But we never knew whether any of the stories we heard were true. Marv never wrote to us again. After that last sad morning with Jake, Marv just kept on going.

Paris, 1966

The Night of the Little Brown Men

He could see them; he could almost smell them, lying there in the darkness, their brown skin and black pyjamas blending into the dark muck of the jungle floor. He lay on his bed in the hot, close room and he could see all the little brown men lying there waiting for the Americans, Glenn Ford, John Wayne, Jimmy Stewart, walking single file up the jungle trail. In a moment, the Americans would be between them and the little brown men would stand up and open fire. They would keep firing until all the impossibly handsome Americans were dead. Then the little brown

97

men would scramble over the bodies picking up the Americans' weapons before they disappeared into the jungle following tracks no white man could ever hope to see.

In the next room, he could hear the crib rocking as the child woke and began to stir. Soon, he knew, his son would begin to cry and his wife would get up from beside him and the day would begin again. In the pale, clear light of morning, he would be all right again. He was sure. He would be able to forget the terrible vision of the little brown men that had wracked him all night. He lit another cigarette and watched the smoke drift up to the ceiling.

What do they want from me? he said. He addressed the ceiling because that was as close as he could bring himself to talking to God. When people asked, he said he was an agnostic but the truth was that he believed in God. He had a theory and he had explained it many times over bottles of Valpolicella and tables filled with empty espresso cups. God, he told his listeners, was the force that made him write music. God is pure creative power. You with your writing, and you over there with your sculpture and me with my music, we are all trying to do God's work on earth. Everything we do is an expression of God. If you wanted to get really sentimental about it, you could almost say we were disciples. God is all around us, you see, in every human being, in every blade of grass, and yes, in every slum street. But only we, the artists, can make the dumb God of nature articulate and so help our fellow human beings on the road upward to pure spirituality.

When they objected, when they accused him of being a pantheist, a pagan even, he did not fight back. He hated to argue. Violence of any kind gave him a migraine headache. Anyway, their criticism never shook his faith. He knew what he knew. The only trouble was that he did not feel able to talk to this God he wrote music for. It seemed to him too humiliating to fall on his knees and ask for God's help. Even when he felt so terribly alone and frightened it was somehow breaking faith with God to ask for comfort. It destroyed the equality of their relationship. So he poured out his troubles to the ceiling of his bedroom.

Why don't they leave me alone? he said. Look, I'm guilty. I confess. Everything the white man did in Africa and Asia for 300 years he did in my name. Okay? I inherit all of it. What more can I do? I can't stop the Americans. They've gone crazy. They don't even talk about right and wrong, or Democracy and Communism anymore. They just go on and on about the agonies of power, their mouths filled all the time with those terrible wooden phrases about responsibility and peace and defending freedom. The Americans are obsessed by the sound of their own voices. They'll kill millions of their own and millions of other people before they'll let one of their myths die. Okay? They're as bad as the Nazis ever were. I admit it. But I can't stop them. There's nothing that I can do. Absolutely nothing.

His wife stirred under the blankets beside him and turned onto her stomach. He reached down to touch her. Her body under the thin cotton nightgown was as warm as toast. He ran his hand over the contours of her back. So thin, a child's body. She was still so much a child. He had been married to her for a whole year and she seemed to grow only more soft and innocent.

What did her world consist of? Her cello. The Victoria String Quartet. Lessons once a week and three hours of rehearsal every day for her Conservatory recital in the fall. Her music and her husband. Her beautiful, hairy-chested, curly-haired husband. Her husband the music teacher, the composer and intellectual. Her music, her husband and now too, the baby. She clutched his hand to the door of the delivery room and the nurse wheeling her blessed them with a warm and patronizing smile. Such children! Two beautiful, talented children playing house together. And look what we did! All by ourselves, look what we did. We made a baby. It was so easy. And the baby, too, was beautiful.

He tried to imagine the songs the little brown men sang as they fired their tommy guns at the Americans. But the only songs he could imagine for them sounded too much like something Pete Seeger might use to serenade an undergraduate audience. Where have all the flowers gone? What have they done to the rain? They've turned it into napalm. That's what they've done. Flaming gas pouring from the sky. And the little brown men were coming to ask him, where were you when the Americans dropped napalm over us? What did you do about the Lazy Dog that spewed deadly metal slivers through our villages?

I was writing music. I wrote three sonatas for harpsichord. I wrote a concerto for flute and piano to celebrate the birth of my son. And right now, I'm working on my first symphony. I come home from the Conservatory every day at four and my wife clears the baby out of the livingroom and somehow puts dampers on the whole apartment and I sit down and work on my symphony until suppertime. I'm an artist. What happens in the outside world is not my concern.

He remembered the day his wife had explained Lester Pearson and he smiled up at the ceiling. Surely God must smile back and bless such tender moments between a man and a woman.

"Lester Pearson is really a conservative," his wife had said. "He shouldn't go around calling himself a Liberal. It's a very dishonest thing for him to do."

He had come home and found her clipping editorials

from the daily newspapers and putting them in one of the folders she always seemed to have around the apartment. He asked her gently why it mattered at all to her what Lester Pearson was.

"Because in the next election I'll be old enough to vote," she had said. "I want to vote for the right man. Lester Pearson says he's a Liberal but really he has a very conservative mind. You can tell that just from reading the papers. You'd be surprised how much you can learn if you read the papers carefully. Pearson doesn't have any ideas different from Diefenbaker. And besides, he lisps."

"Don't blame me," he had said. "I voted for Tommy Douglas, remember?"

"You vote the way your father always voted," she had said. "That doesn't count."

"You're a musician," he had said. "You shouldn't care what a lot of crooked politicians do."

"Oh you're so wrong," she had said. "I can't tell you how wrong you are." She touched his heart when she was angry and trying to be serious. "Serious" was one of her favourite words. "Marriage," she liked to say, "is a very serious business." At least once a week she sat down and gave him a detailed analysis of how she thought their relationship was progressing.

"Politics are part of life," she had said. "Nothing human should ever be alien to us. I've heard you say that yourself at least a hundred times."

She was wrong, of course, especially about why he voted socialist. But he would not spoil the moment by getting into a political argument with her. He hated arguments of any kind. The truth was he had voted socialist because socialism was Good. He believed in Good just as he believed in God. God smiled down on the world and offered the occasional word of encouragement, especially to artists, but it was the Good things that made the world livable and kept it running smoothly. Unemployment Insurance was Good. A redistribution of wealth was Good. Medicare was Good. The CBC was Good and the Canada Council was Good, although it could be better and give more money to individual musicians instead of always to institutions like the ballet and the symphony orchestras that had their own organizations for raising funds. A better break for French-Canadians was Good; Nuclear Disarmament was Good, Robert Fulford was Good. The ecumenical movement was Good. Sex was Good, food and wine were Good and even a little whisky once in a while was Good. Painting was Good and writing was Good and music was Good. He was Good although he knew that at times he still had bad thoughts. Sometimes he wished his son had never been conceived and sometimes he wished he had not married so young. But he was learning to face up to his bad thoughts and make them turn and go away. He knew he was basically a Good man and he was trying all the time to be better. He would always try.

Surely that all counts for something, he said. But how do I explain it to the little brown men? Do they even have a word for it in their strange, five-tone language? He thought not. History was the only thing the little brown men understood. History does not reward virtue and punish evil. History is impersonal. History bestows power on whoever is first in line to receive it. The little brown men understood that history was on their side. What the white men liked to call their Western Civilization was dying on its feet. The white men, the Americans, were fighting now only to preserve their wealth. And this was not enough; wealth is not worth that much killing and dying for. The Americans laboured under a dead weight of guilt. They knew their time was up but they would not admit it. History had deserted them, but they refused to even utter the words. Their fighting back only prolonged the collective agony of the world. Stupid, stupid Americans!

He could see the little brown men moving silently under the jungle trees. They were spread out, advancing on a broad front like Robin Hood's men through the forest of Nottingham. He imagined that his bed lay in an exposed clearing and they were coming for him. What did they want? How much could they ask of him? How much were they entitled to ask?

Outside the bedroom venetian blinds, he could see the sky beginning to grow light. He stubbed out the cigarette and moaned. The moan stirred his wife. She raised herself on one elbow, turned a bleary eye on him and then sank back into sleep again. What a miserable day this was going to be, he told himself. A full schedule of classes lay ahead; nine to three in the afternoon, harmony, ear training, composition and three private piano students. Only twenty minutes to wolf down his sandwiches in the Conservatory cafeteria. And even when he came home, he would have to face the piano for two hours. Most days, he just doodled for the first hour, improvising to fool his wife so that she would keep the baby away from him. It was usually 5:30 by the time he began getting any real work done and by the time he felt he was really starting to get something worthwhile down on paper, it was six o'clock and time to eat supper.

Did the little brown men hate him? Just because his skin was white? What kind of world did the little brown men really want? He thought of it as a world to be filled by not-quite people. All his traditions, the books, the music, the architecture, the very language that he breathed in and out every day, "soul, spirit, sensitivity, self-expression," had taught him to glorify the individual. The only real evil in his world was to have potential and not fulfil it. To have the talent to become a composer or an artist or even a good chartered accountant and to stifle this ability, or to allow it to be stifled, was a crime against nature. It was an affront to God. The Renaissance man, the explorers and conquistadors; John Wayne leading a cattle drive up to Abilene. But this kind of individualism had now carried the world to the brink of anarchy. He saw that clearly now. The days of the Great Men were over. They had played their role in history. They had carried the world from just beyond the stone age to the edge of the electronic wonderland where the many-tongued and armed computers would do the work that had once been the lot of human slaves and then fallen to the industrial proletariat. It was just another of history's monstrous jokes that the ancient dream of almost unlimited leisure for everybody should be almost within reach just when the world was falling apart.

The trouble was that the Great Men needed room to work in. And now there was almost no room left in the world. The population had exploded; every newspaper carried some new and horrifying statistical forecast of what the world would be like in the year 2000. Only a special kind of man, one who had long ago surrendered all his private dreams to the collective need, could survive in this new, overcrowded world. The Chinese understood this and had turned themselves into insects, marching every day to the fields and factories in their identical blue cotton uniforms. Millions and millions of blue ants swarming over the face of the world. They never talked about such things as "sensitivity" and "self-expression" because such things were no longer needed and in fact, did not exist in their world. The Chinese had learned to be collective human beings. The little brown men had learned too.

They would inherit the earth because they were the people best prepared to live on it. "Collectivize," that was the idea history had given them. Time was on their side. They knew they were going to win.

I should help them, he told himself. I should get on the right side of history. It's still not too late. Already in the newspapers, there was talk of international brigades. He tried to imagine himself as one of those tender young men he had once seen in a photograph on the cover of a record of Spanish Civil War songs. It was a snapshot, torn and brown around the edges, and he imagined it had been found on the body of some dead soldier. The picture had upset and frightened him. So much waste! How many Good things would those young men have had time to do if they had not gone to fight in Spain? Perhaps one of them was a genius, another Mozart or Beethoven. In the picture, they were all holding their rifles the same way, stock on the ground, barrels held loosely to one side of their hips. Bandoliers were slung across their bodies, and on their shoulders they carried thin blanket rolls. He was sure the picture had been taken in the early morning because all the soldiers looked so cold. Their lips seemed to be breathing out frost. They were all in a line, waiting to go somewhere. Probably to the front. They were going out to die.

Hungary, he said to the ceiling, I almost went to Hungary. For those few days between the time the revolution began and the time the Russian tanks finally rolled into Budapest, he had been sure that Hungary was going to be the Spain of his generation. An ad appeared in the newspapers. Volunteers who came to an address in a seedy, immigrant section of the city would be flown to Vienna and conveyed across the frontier to join the Freedom Fighters. In 1936, the Good fight had been alongside the Communists; in 1956, it had looked as though the Good fight was going to be against the Communists.

But the principle was the same, he had told himself. Freedom of the individual was in jeopardy; the barbarians were at the gates. But it was all happening at a bad time for him. He was taking private harp and oboe lessons to improve his command over the orchestra, and he had to study hard to hold onto his scholarship. He was methodically preparing himself to earn a living teaching so that he could write music.

But he was still a single man and without responsibilities except to his art. Duty was calling him loudly and brutally. He stopped going to classes and wandered up and down the campus, arguing with himself and wondering what made him hesitate to join the volunteers. He blamed his selfish, egotistical, pampered, middle-class soul. He went to an open-air prayer meeting on the campus. Speaker after speaker denounced the Communist treachery. One man with a thick European accent broke down and had to be led weeping from the microphone. A United Church minister led them all in singing "Onward Christian Soldiers." He sang with the others, bareheaded in the grey, October afternoon. This must have been what the world was like in 1938, he told himself. But still he did not join the volunteers.

Then the revolution collapsed. There was no more talk of international brigades to help the Hungarian Freedom Fighters. He saw that he had been right to hesitate. The revolution had not been all that it had seemed at first. As the long newspaper and magazine stories and the book about those few, fiery days in Budapest began to appear, he discovered that there had been Fascists among the Freedom Fighters. Not many, it was true, but enough to made the Good cause not so Good after all. What if the Freedom Fighters had won the revolution and then the Fascists had won control of the country from the Freedom Fighters? What if he had gone to Hungary and given his life to help instal a Fascist regime that was worse than that of Stalinists? No, he told himself, it was still better to be cautious when dealing with causes. After all, hadn't many of the men who went to Spain returned home bitter and disillusioned?

But what about the peace movement? That was a pure, idealistic cause if ever there was one.

I'll join the ban-the-bombers if they come and ask me to, he said. I'll even go on parades with them and all that sort of thing. But so far, they don't seem to need me. And I've got all my music to think about. I'm trying to make the world a better place with my music. Surely a composer is worth as much as somebody carrying a placard down the street. Beethoven could have been a soldier too, you know. He believed that Napoleon was going to be the great saviour of Europe. Well then, he should have joined Napoleon's armies. It was the logical thing to do. Nobody holds it against Beethoven that he stayed home and wrote music.

He could hear birds now. Their shrill cries amazed him. It had never occurred to him before that there were birds in the city, birds that sang to each other in the mornings. But then he had never, in his whole life, been awake at this hour before. He believed in sleep. Sleep was Good. Artists must keep themselves in good physical condition. He walked to and from the Conservatory every day except when it was raining or too bitterly cold. And he always got at least seven hours' sleep every night. When his wife woke up, he would tell her about his discovery. Birds sang outside their apartment house. Their chirruping sounds were immensely, almost absurdly reassuring. They were the tongues of the great life force, the holy spirit infusing every living thing. It was part of what he was trying to articulate in his music. Above all else, he was an artist. An artist's first duty was to create.

How did the little brown men manage to make sandals from old tires? Tires were curved. The sandals must be curved too. How did they fit over the feet of the little brown men? Why did the newspapers always say they wore black pyjamas? If they wore them during the day to fight in, what did they sleep in at night? How did they make their clothes? Did they have sewing-machines? Did they have whole pyjama factories hidden away in the jungle?

They were coming now. They padded silently over the jungle paths. They swung through the trees like Tarzan. They climbed out of the paddy fields, their faces and clothing covered with muck and slime, and swarmed like insects over the dry hills. But I can't stop the Americans, he said. I can't help you! You can't ask anything from me! But the faces of the little brown men remained hard and unmoved. He realized with a withering horror that they did not even see him. Their black, liquid eyes swept past him as though he did not exist, had never existed. As though nothing of him, his life, his way of life, stood in their path. Up close, their faces looked astonishingly western, as though the ghosts of white men lived inside those brown skins. They're just like me, he thought. It was almost his last thought. I'm a musician, he whispered to them. I write music to make the world a better place to live in. They were over him. They were past him. They swept on as though he had never existed. As though Beethoven and Brahms and Bach and Debussy and Shostakovich had never existed. Ten thousand years of history, ten thousand years of men painfully learning to accumulate and organize and systematize their experience so that he could come and in a few years, three for his BA, two for his MA, retrace all the steps of all the musicians who had gone before him and hold all their experience and knowledge inside him so that he could be ready to advance the world one more step along and upward toward God. It was all gone in an instant. Trampled under the rubber-tired soles of the little brown men.

"The baby," his wife said. She jumped from the bed, instantly awake, and ran into the next room. The blankets caught and held her nightgown for a moment and he caught a glimpse of her long legs, still white and moist from sleep. They reassured him. He was going to be all right and he was going to look after her too. He saw clearly the way out now. It was almost too simple. He sat up in the bed and lit another cigarette. Sweat poured down the matted fur of his chest.

"Poor kiddo, he's soaking wet," his wife said. She came into the bedroom, holding the baby in the crook of her arms, swinging the bundle gently. The baby cried bitterly. His son sounded startlingly old to him. Sobs wracked and choked the tiny body. His son bawled in rage and insatiable frustration.

"Didn't you hear him?" his wife said.

"No, I'm sorry."

"Are you feeling all right? You don't look so good."

"I couldn't fall asleep. I've been up most of the night."

"Poor baby," his wife said. She shifted her son awkwardly in her arms so she could bend over the bed and kiss her husband on the cheek.

"Go back to sleep," she said. "I'll take kiddo into the next room and change him there. We won't disturb you any more."

"It's morning already," he said. "I should get up now."

"You can sleep for an hour still," his wife said. "I'll wake you and I'll have breakfast all ready when you get up. You can be out of the house in half an hour. You've got to get some rest, honey. I insist."

Drained and weary now and grateful to his wife, he sank back into the bed and pulled the covers over his head to blot out the morning light. He felt warm and comfortable and very sure of himself. The emotional crisis had passed. The fever had broken and he felt himself empty of all emotion and a little light-headed. The little brown men no longer frightened him. He was going to sign a peace treaty with them.

It struck him that what he was about to do was, in fact, total and abject surrender. For an instant, resentment flickered inside him and threatened to burst into an angry tirade. But he quenched this feeling. Surrender was the only way. There was no fighting history.

I resign all concepts of the Good, he said through the blankets that covered his face. I accept freely and willingly and being in sound mind and body my guilt for everything the Americans have done or are going to do. I accept that everything I believe in is a product of the rise of the mercantile class and the industrial revolution. I will never be able to see the world, never even be able to distinguish between right and wrong or good and bad except through the distorting lenses of my own narrow class interest. Now the time has come for the class of the little brown men. I step aside for them. I pat them on the shoulder as they go by and wish them well. There is no objective truth now. Love is a bourgeois luxury. Only historical laws are objective. Historical necessity will shape truth to suit the needs of the moment. Good is relative. Beauty is a matter of opinion. The next class, surging now to power, will decide what is beautiful. That is their privilege. Yes, it is one of the spoils of victory. I know, I accept. I am ready to be swept under the giant, impersonal waves of history. The best a sane man can do in these times is surrender with dignity, and grace. Grace, that was it. The idea pleased him. Grace. Hemingway would have understood.

That ought to hold them for a while, he said to the ceiling. It takes time to clean out the mind. The little brown men ought to show a little sympathy for him. He was trying very hard. But he didn't expect the little brown men to really understand him. His only hope was that by surrendering to them and getting out of their way, he would be left alone to continue to write his music. He didn't expect the little brown men to like, or even listen to, his music after they had taken over the world. But maybe in a few generations, when their bitterness had subsided and their society was becoming more wealthy and leisurely, they would become curious about the people who had gone before them and some musicologist or historian would uncover his works and they would be played. It was a poor kind of immortality to hope for. Beethoven would have scorned it. But times had changed. A man had to take what he could get. And by surrendering, at least he could hope to go on composing.

The sound of music startled him. And then he realized where the sound was coming from and he relaxed again. His wife was playing her cello to soothe the baby. Automatically his mind catalogued the sound; the largo from Bach's sixth suite for unaccompanied cello. It was one of the pieces his wife was to play at her Conservatory recital.

He signed the articles of surrender on the deck of the USS *Missouri*. General MacArthur was there and Admiral Nimitz and even old Bull Halsey. They stood together in their crisp, khaki uniforms, hard, sunburned men who disdained to even look at him. John Wayne was there with his son Patrick. John Wayne was looking at him as though he were some kind of renegade Indian. What a cowardly thing to do, John Wayne seemed to be saying. What an unmanly thing to be doing! The little brown men who swarmed so thickly over the ship they seemed to be a sea of black pyjamas still kept a reasonable distance from John Wayne and the two Colt '44s he wore at his hips. The little brown men pushed the articles of surrender at him across the table. Without even bothering to read them, he signed.

He felt very tired now. It was the pleasant, physical weariness that comes at the end of a good job well done. He pushed the blankets down from his face, rolled over and sought a cool section of the pillow to rest his cheek against. He seemed to be sinking slowly into a profound happiness. It surrounded him like a tepid, pleasant bath. He fell asleep.

London, 1965

Back Where I Can Be Me

"I wanna go back, where I can be me, to the Bonjour Tristesse Brassiere Companee,

"I wanna go back, where I can be free, to the Bee Jay Tristesse Brassiere Factoree...."

She was still singing it when I got back to the flat and I told her, Kate, if you keep that up I'm going to beat the hell out of you, so help me God I will. But she just kept going, tucking the sheets around the corners of the bed, our bed, and I tried to imagine her sleeping alone in it tonight. And the night after that and how long would it be until someone else was in there where I had been for, God, it was almost two years now.

"I wanna go back where I can be me, at the Bonjour Tristesse Brassiere Companee."

I sat down on the bed and hauled her across my knee and spanked her. I pulled her pants down and hit her hard enough to leave fingerprints on her behind. Afterward, she stood in front of me rubbing the pain away and telling me what a juvenile fool I was to think I could solve all my problems with violence. Anyway, she said, what did it matter? In 24 hours I would be back in Toronto, good old Tee-oh, welcome back little man. Give my regards to the Park Plaza, will you? And Yorkville and if you see my mother, I'm sure you'll pay a duty call on my mother, tell her I still think she's a silly old bitch.

I went into the kitchen and poured myself a drink. I used up the last of our precious bottle of Scotch and that pleased me. A scorched-earth policy. I was leaving nothing behind in London that Kate could use. Kate came and kissed me. She hugged me; it was awkward and clumsy with me still sitting in the chair trying to keep my drink from spilling and finally, she sank to her knees beside me and rested her head in my lap.

"I'm glad you're going," she said. "You won't believe me, but I think you're doing the right thing."

"Why?"

"You're a loser," she said. "I only suspected it before I started living with you but I know it for sure now. You ought to get some analysis when you get home. I know you keep saying it's all nonsense but really you're just afraid of it. You think if they get you all straightened out, you won't be able to act any more. But you can't act worth a shit now and six months with a good headshrinker might be enough to get you functioning again. Anyway, you'll be better off in Toronto than you ever were in London. At home you've got your friends and your family and they'll look after you. They'll keep you from falling on your ass so much."

"What are you going to do?"

"You still think some man is going to jump into bed with me as soon as you get on the plane, don't you? You'd like to kill me for that, wouldn't you? Strangle me. Hit me over the head with a hammer."

"I've still got a couple of hours before I leave for the airport. All I still have to do is put my shirts in the suitcase."

"All right," Kate said. "What the hell? Why not? Only try not to be so quick on the trigger, eh? Let me have one last fond remembrance of you."

She was lying naked on the bed by the time I finished my drink and joined her. I undressed slowly, sitting beside her, and hung my pants carefully over the chair. She gave me a drag on her cigarette and I lay down beside her. We stared at the ceiling, each waiting for the other person to begin. Come home with me, Kate. You can make more dough teaching school in Toronto and you can have a better life. We'll go middle class. I'll marry you and buy a suit. What the hell? We started there and the sooner we get back where we belong and get on with it, the better off we're going to be. But what the hell? What's the use? I'd been saying it every day for three months. Oh no, not again! Here we go again! Every day you sound more and more like my old bitch mother. Kate turned on her elbow to look at me. Would it help to say I love you, Kate?

"I love you, Kate," I said.

She lay there looking at me, a beautiful, white porcelain blank. Her body was thin and hard and cruel; the bones stuck out. It was an uncomfortable body to lie on. Only a man who loved Kate would put up with that sharp little pelvis cutting like a knife across his stomach.

"You're a good piece of ass," I said.

She smiled and pulled me to her. So what is life? *Toujours gai.* So what is love? *Toujours gai.* When the one great scorer comes to write against your name, he writes not how you won or lost but how many times you scored. It was time to go home. I knew it and I was going home. I could feel the handwriting on my bones. I'd written my sister to borrow money for an airplane ticket. Oh yes, do come home, everyone will be so pleased. It was time for Kate too, but she was too stubborn. It's not that I have anything against Canada, you understand, it's just that I couldn't live any more without the National Film Theatre and the Sunday papers. People at home are so screwed up. Getting their heads shrunk, getting divorces. But look at me, I'm so free in London. Wheee! I can be myself in London. Goodbye Kate. Cheers Kate. I love you Kate.

"Oh God," Kate said.

The doorbell shattered us. We stopped and lay still, waiting for it to go away. It rang again. We were afraid to move, afraid that even the rustling sheets would give us away. The doorbell shattered us again and this time there was a loud knocking too. It sounded as though someone was trying to break our door down.

"Answer it," Kate said.

"Why?" I said. "Whoever it is, I don't want to see them."

"You don't live here any more," Kate said. "It must be someone for me."

"I haven't finished yet," I said.

"Well, I haven't even got properly started yet," Kate said. "Answer the door and get rid of them and then come back and we'll start all over again. We'll get two rides for the price of one."

I pulled on my clothes and went to the door. Howie

hung in the door frame, a symphony in blue. Blue Chelsea boots, powder-blue slacks, navy-blue shirt, turquoise ascot with white polka dots. He had a bottle of scotch cradled in his arm.

"Bonjour," Howie said. "I came to get you to the plane on time."

I took him into the kitchen, what else could I do? and we broke open his bottle and mixed it with ice. Howie was very happy.

"I've got a part in a telly series," he said. "Thirteen weeks. It's called the 'Guns of Sicily.' It's all about vigilante types who run about fighting the Mafia. I play the leader's kid brother. Not bad, eh? Thirteen weeks."

"Ciao," I said.

"I know, I know," Howie said. "I ought to be going back into rep. Do some more Shakespeare and all that. But it's been a cold winter and I can use some money. I need new clothes and I want to fix up my flat. Buy a fridge and rent a TV set. Maybe I'll go into rep when the series is over. After all, it's only thirteen weeks."

Kate came in. She was wearing a bright orange dress and a pink scarf. She had tied her hair back with a pink ribbon and scrubbed her face. Howie poured her some scotch.

"Congratulations, Howie," she said. "I heard you from the bedroom. It sounds pretty good."

"It is pretty good," Howie said. "Well, here's to the Mafia."

"Let's go for a walk," Kate said.

We wheeled across Hampstead Heath. Warty Spanish *au pair* girls clumped by, pushing prams. Flower children, their army-surplus jackets stapled with plastic flowers, rushed up and presented us with tulips pillaged from somebody's garden. Howie gave them an elaborate Shakespearean bow. Kate giggled. We watched little boys in grey flannel shorts playing soccer, tripping each other, bouncing the ball off their heads. We went to the Portobello market and Kate bought me an old silver cigarette holder for a going-away present. We rummaged through carts filled with junk looking for a picture for Howie's wall but they were all too expensive. We took the ferry from Westminster down to Putney. Chelsea, Battersea and Fulham glided by. We sat in the front drinking Bass ale from cans. On the Putney Embankment, a City man was feeding swans. He wore a black pin-stripe suit and vest and a bowler and carried an umbrella over his arm. He had a paper bag and he took hunks of bread out of it and threw them to the swans. Winston Churchill is alive in Argentina. One of the swans rose up, flapped its wings and walked along the water. Kate said he looked like a helicopter. Howie said it was impossible to tell the sex of swans. He'd read about it in the *Guardian*. The scientists were having trouble. Showers came, a London rain, warm and thin. We rested our chins on a brick wall and watched an old lady working in her garden. She wore a yellow plastic raincoat and a big black fisherman's hat. Her garden was filled with pear trees and rose bushes. They intertwined above her head. The garden was thick and lush, a bit of jungle beside the Hammersmith railway tracks. Heavy little girls in psychedelic miniskirts formed a circle around Howie. The leader blew a whistle and they tripped lightly around him singing "Britannia rules the Waves." Kate and I rested beside a street-lamp. It was dusk and the lamp covered us with a weird orange light. A wet, mouldy smell rose from the river. The sun came out again. The air was green and bright again. We went to Hyde Park and watched the girls row the boys along the Serpentine. We walked over the rolling hills to Speakers' Corner and bought Eskimo Pies from the Wall's Ice Cream truck. The anarchists and the Communists and even the Salvation Army were talking about Vietnam. We went to hear our favourite, the black nationalist who'd lost his hands. He spoke from the top of a ladder. A piece of black velvet had been folded over the top to make a lectern. He called the English white monkeys and pounded his stumps on the top of the ladder until the blood came. Who invented perfume? The French invented perfume. Who buys all the perfume the French can make? The English buy all the perfume. The white men stink. Black men smell sweet all the time. Black men are beautiful.

"I'm going to have a stage name," Howie said. "Hawk."

"Howard Hawk?" I said. "You'll never get away with it. He'll sue you."

"Nigel," Howie said. "It's going to be Nigel Hawk."

"It sounds bent to me," Kate said. "You're not getting that way, are you Howie? That would be too bad."

"I don't like it either," Howie said. "I've been fighting with my agent now for three weeks. I keep telling him, Trevor, I'm not a Nigel. It's just not me. But he says I need the name to get work. If I don't use it, he'll drop me. He got me the audition for the Mafia series."

"Well, it's something to look forward to at home," I said. "I want to be there when your father gets the first letter signed, 'Nigel Hawk.'"

We stopped at a pub and I had a final pint of Guinness. The pub was hoked-up Edwardian. We sat on red velvet settees surrounded by chandeliers and gilt mirrors. The pub filled up with Earl's Court types, pink, cheeky faces in turtle-neck sweaters and ratty tweed jackets. Vinegary English accents washed over us.

"You people should be coming with me," I said. "Mark my words, you'll both be back within a year."

"I don't want to go home a failure," Howie said. "I'll wait

until I've done some good things here and got something of a name. Then I'll take a trip home and look around. If I go back now, I'm a nothing and nobody's going to give me any work."

"I don't want to go back at all," Kate said. "Period, the hell with it."

"You're both cowards," I said.

"So are you," Howie said. "So are you."

We went back to the flat. Kate and I went into the bedroom to finish my packing and we made love. Howie waited for us in the kitchen, drinking his Teacher's Highland Cream. We took a cab to the Gloucester Road air terminal. The cab swung up the ski-slide ramp and dropped me at "Departures." Howie and Kate came too. They waited while I stood in line to check my suitcase. The girl in the red Air Canada suit stamped my ticket and gave me a boarding pass. Howie and I shook hands and then we embraced. Goodbye. Good luck, old cock. Kate kissed me on the cheek and then on the mouth. Goodbye. Take care, take care.

And that, kids, is how I came home to Canada. Listen! Mommy's calling. She's got some Borden's chocolate milk and bread and jam for you. Run along now. Scoot.

London, 1967

The Demonstration

If there was one shared experience that united all of us who came of age politically during the sixties, it was being at a demonstration.

People took to the streets with placards and banners for all sorts of reasons, from banning the bomb to winning for black people their civil rights and a bit of dignity to legalizing marijuana.

I first went to demonstrations as a reporter for Maclean's Magazine. *I covered the first attempt by the non-violent nuclear disarmament movement to use the non-violent methods of Martin Luther King and Gandhi in Canada. They blockaded a Bomarc Missile base at La Macaza, Quebec.*

I tried to deal with that demonstration as a narrator, outside the action, in my first novel, Scratch One Dreamer.

In the spring of 1968, I went to New York for the old Star Weekly *and I covered the assassinations of Martin Luther King and Bobby Kennedy. In the summer, I began to hang out on the lower east side with the Youth International Party, the Yippies.*

The Democrats had scheduled their national convention for August in Chicago. The National Mobilization to End the War in Vietnam, or "Mobe" as we called it, and the Yippies scheduled demonstrations for the same time. The police tried to stop them and there were fearsome riots in the parks and streets.

I went to cover the demonstrations for the Toronto Star *and I lived with one of the Yippie organizers. By the end of the week, I was wearing a purple Yippie button and I was just another crazy freak running in the streets. I wrote a book about that experience called* Living the Revolution: The Yippies in Chicago.

By the spring of 1969, the "V for Victory" sign had been replaced by the clenched fist. People I knew talked only of violence. Some of them wound up in jail for planting bombs.

I came back to Toronto. I didn't really believe that much in "the revolution" any more. If I absolutely had to "pick up the gun," as we used to say, I decided I'd better do it in Toronto where I knew lots of good places to hide. It was the beginning of being a Canadian nationalist.

I tried to put the surreal feeling of the end of the New Left and the demonstration years into a surreal novel: My Sexual and Other Revolutions.

1

A cold summer shower had begun by three o'clock, the time scheduled for the assault on the base. The sun still shone overhead, dazzling as cut-glass, but underneath it, the thin, chill rain drenched the double line of vigilers at the RCAF base. It washed over their placards, and the painted slogans began to melt and run down onto the asphalt. So many people had now turned out to vigil that they packed both sides of the road leading from the main highway to the guard hut and gate pole. Two nervous provincial policemen patrolled between them, wearing holstered pistols and carrying billies.

Kelly stepped out of the line of vigilers and came to the centre of the road.

"It's time," he called out into the rain. "Would all those going on the CD step out now and join me at the highway. And please, all you people on the vigil, whatever happens, don't break ranks and for God's sake don't come to the gate."

Standing just behind the vigilers where their line met the highway, Joe counted 23 people coming out for the act of civil disobedience. There were eighteen boys and five girls, all dressed in blue jeans. They had not expected the rain; they shivered in their thin cotton shirts. The group gathered around Kelly and Macadam, and a provincial policeman came too. He warned them that the land beyond the highway was federal property and the responsibility of the air-force police, but that if anything happened on the highway, he would be forced to arrest them. Kelly thanked him for the warning and the policemen left.

"Now everybody knows what to do," Kelly said. "We don't have to talk any more. I'm going down to the gate for a last word with the air-force police. When I come back, we'll all go down the road together in a single line."

And then, overcome, Kelly raised his arms over them in blessing and exultation.

"It's going to work," he shouted, the rain streaming down his face. "It's really going to work."

The group formed a long, uneven line, and Kelly set off alone down the aisle of vigilers to talk to the air-force police at the gate. Joe watched him go, feeling frightened for Kelly, frightened for all of them and at the same time, absurdly, chokingly proud. The rain had soaked through Kelly's white cotton shirt, and now it clung in wrinkles to his back, like a piece of sodden, transparent paper.

This is not a revolution. Joe repeated the words desperately to himself until they became a slogan. This is not a revolution. This is just a collection of university students who do not yet understand how old and tired and immovable the real world is. Nothing that happens on this road will matter. The world will never hear about these people. They will go to jail and the bombs will stay inside the base ready to be used. The spirit these children show so bravely now will go stale and wither and disappear into the prickly limbo of all causes that were too clean and too good. But the bombs here and the bombs all over the world will still remain. Joe felt a hand slip inside his. Boag had left the line of vigilers and come up beside him. She held his hand now behind his back. She squeezed hard, digging her fingers into him.

Kelly came back down the road and called the marchers together.

"The air-force cops are all behind the pole," he told them. "They've formed a line right across the road. They're going to try and block us, but they won't arrest anyone unless we manage to get over onto the other side of the pole. We'll try to push our way through. If any of the cops grabs for you, sink to the ground and go limp. Okay? Everybody into a single line again. We'll spread out when we reach the pole. This is it, people. This is really it."

The demonstrators began to march slowly down the road. Then the shouts rang out.

"Stop!"

"Wait for us!"

"Hold it!"

Four men came flailing down the road. Klaus, the German boy, recognized them and ran out to meet them. They embraced Klaus and he brought them to Kelly and Macadam. Joe saw, to his astonishment, that one of them wore a clerical collar. They were from the Student Christian Movement in Toronto, and Klaus had written them about the demonstration. They had set out the night before but their car had broken down and they had just now reached the base. The police had made them park up the road and they had run the last mile. Now they wanted to commit civil disobedience with the rest.

"But you don't know the plans," Macadam warned them. "You don't know what we're going to do. You don't even have jail kits."

Joe saw the policemen beginning to cross the road to see what the delay was. He pulled Boag closer to him to try to shield her from the driving rain.

"Klaus told us the general idea," the minister said. He had a round pink face, still lined with baby fat that bulged over his still-white collar, and blond, curly hair. "Anything else you can explain while we're going down the road."

"More bodies," Kelly said. "What harm can they do? We've got to get going for God's sake!"

"What seems to be the trouble now?" the policeman asked Macadam.

"No trouble at all, sir," Macadam said. "We're starting now."

The line started to move again. Joe began to feel now the emotional power of the vigil. As the marchers passed between the double line of boys and girls with their smeared and dripping placards, the vigilers became more than witnesses. Because they had willed to be there, they were now partaking of the action. What was about to happen at the gate was about to happen to them too. The marchers began to sing, softly at first, and then with growing power. The vigilers joined in and the song rose, hoarse and defiant, over the rainswept road.

> We are not afraid,
> We are not afraid,
> We are not afraid toda-a-ay
> Oh deep in my heart,
> I do believe,
> We are not afraid today.

> We'll walk hand in hand
> We'll walk hand in hand
> We'll walk hand in hand some da-a-ay
> Oh deep in my heart,
> I do believe
> We'll walk hand in hand some day.

At the gate, Kelly and Macadam turned and went to opposite sides of the road. The marchers spread out between them. The song died away. In cold, total silence, the thin line of demonstrators advanced against the wall of police.

The police had locked arms. As the demonstrators met them, they threw out their legs to block them. Joe saw Macadam trying to force his way between two policemen. Another ran behind the line and pushed Macadam in the face, throwing him back from the pole. Macadam tried again; he threw himself at a policeman's chest. Kelly had managed to work his way between two policemen, but they pinned him between their shoulders. And Kelly could not lift himself over the pole. He was held helpless, his legs thrashing in the air.

Some of the marchers tried to duck under the pole. The sergeant ran behind the line of legs, bending over to push back at the faces and shoulders of the marchers. One girl managed to slip through at the end and stand up on the inside of the pole. Two policemen ran to her and grabbed her by the arms. She sank down and lay curled in a foetal ball on the wet asphalt. This is it, Joe thought. The first arrest! The line of vigilers seemed to hang in stricken silence, waiting to see what the air-force police would do with the girl who lay huddled at their feet.

They did nothing. Three policemen formed a wall around her. Their legs blocked her from moving any farther into the base. But they did not touch her. The marchers took a step back and then, almost as one man, they advanced against the impassive bodies and locked arms of the air-force police. But every hole had been blocked. They could not move.

Then, suddenly, Brock sat down on the road. He was so close to the line that his folded legs touched the boots of the policeman in front of him. Joe saw Kelly, still pinned helplessly between the shoulders of the two policemen, look over at Brock and grin. Kelly wriggled free and sat down too. Then one by one, the whole line of marchers sat down facing the police. Only the girl had managed to get beyond the pole. Now she too uncurled and sat up to face the knees of the three policemen who walled her off. The police took a step forward, trying to force the marchers back. For a frightening moment they seemed about to trample the crossed legs below them. Then the sergeant shouted an order and the police stepped back. The march on the base had sunk into a stalemate.

"Is everyone all right?" Kelly's voice rang out over the huddled, soaking marchers.

One by one they called out their replies. They were wet and they were cold but no-one had been hurt.

"We've got to hold a meeting," Kelly said. He spoke quietly now. "We've got to decide what to do next. And we want all you air-force policemen to listen and if you have anything to say, please, by all means join in. We hold our meeting in front of you like this because we are not a secret society. We come to you in a spirit of friendship and love. We want you to know everything we are thinking and everything we are planning to do."

Boag squeezed Joe's hand and began to laugh.

"They're out of their fucking minds," she whispered in his ear. "Kelly will be calling meetings on doomsday."

Klaus led the group that argued for a continued assault on the line of police until they either broke through or forced the police to arrest them for trying. Brock, the American, agreed. They had come here to do more than just lie across the road, he said. Besides, if they didn't get arrested soon, everyone was going to die of pneumonia. Macadam said he too wanted to keep trying to enter the base. He had come to make a personal witness and to stop now would be letting the air force have their own way.

"Does anyone from the air-force base have anything they'd like to say?" Kelly asked.

The sergeant, his three stripes standing out on the sleeve of his blue trench coat, came from behind the line of air-force police. Kelly stood up to shake hands but the sergeant ignored him.

"We can arrest you any time we choose," he told the group. "You were on federal property the minute you left the highway. But we're willing to make an arrangement with you. If you'll make that girl come back onto this side of the pole, we'll let you stay here. For the time being, anyway."

"We can't make her do anything," Kelly said. "This is a democratic organization and everybody acts according to their own conscience. But we'll certainly take what you've said into consideration."

"You're in charge here, I take it," the sergeant said.

"I'm the co-chairman of the group," Kelly said. "The other chairman is over there."

He pointed to Macadam sitting at the other end of the line.

"These men are under strict orders not to talk to anyone in the group," the sergeant said. "If you have anything to say that concerns them, you'll say it to me."

"I'm sorry sir," Kelly said. "But we simply couldn't make a promise like that."

The sergeant swung on his heel and took up a position beside the road, facing his own men.

The meeting continued and now the argument turned in favour of staying. Sooner or later, the air force was going to have to use this road and then the police would have to arrest them. Keeping up the assault was really being unfair to the police. The marchers were forcing them to use violence and that was against all their pacifist principles. Under the stern eye of the sergeant, the policemen gazed stonily over the heads of the marchers.

Kelly called for a vote. The marchers were fifteen to eight in favour of staying where they were. That left only the problem of the girl on the wrong side of the pole. Kelly called another vote and the marchers were in favour of her coming back. But she was in favour of staying where she was, and only an impassioned speech from Kelly convinced her to slide along the ground until she was back in line with the others. The policemen filled the gap in their line.

"You policemen can take it easy for a while if you want," Kelly said. "We're not going anywhere. You have our word on that."

The sergeant gave the at-ease order. The air-force police dropped their lined arms and clasped their hands behind their backs.

"You fellows certainly look a lot more comfortable now," Kelly said. No emotion, not even a sign that they had heard him, showed on the faces of the police. Kelly started to sing.

> We shall not,
> We shall not be moved.
> We shall not,
> We shall not be moved.
> Just like a tree that's standing by the wa-a-ter,
> We shall not be moved.

The vigilers picked up the song and the raucous music roared back and forth along the road. Joe heard Boag singing beside him and then he began to sing too.

> We shall not,
> We shall not be moved.
> We shall not,
> We shall not be moved.
> Just like a tree that's standing by the wa-a-ter,
> We shall not be moved.

The stalemate had ended. The siege had begun.

Paris, 1965

Z

THURSDAY: I woke up in the double bed beside Ken, the *Newsreel* photographer, and discovered that he had an artificial leg. I had fallen asleep in the car, and when we reached the apartment, the *Newsreel* people had pushed me toward a bedroom and said, "In there." Someone was already in one half of the bed and I flopped down on the other half without even bothering to take off my clothes. When I rolled over and opened my eyes a couple of hours later, Ken was fitting on his leg. I looked at the ceiling, the wall, at anything but Ken. I had noticed before that he had a limp, but it was so slight that I'd never even thought about it. Ken had been in Old Town most of the night. The National Guard had moved to Lincoln Park and there had been skirmishing up and down Wells Street, but nothing like the carnage we had heard about down in Grant Park. I stopped trying to look away and watched, fascinated, while Ken fiddled with the buckles and harness on his hip. What the hell? He didn't seem to be embarrassed by it. Why should I be? We were all brothers.

I called Jay at work. She and her boyfriend had managed to get away from Michigan Avenue and home to Willow Street without trouble.

A young couple owned the apartment. He was taking a Ph.D. in education and she was already teaching school. And, obviously, someone was helping them along. The apartment did indeed have seven rooms and all of them were comfortably furnished.

The young couple had been at the Pentagon, but they weren't involved too much in the movement in Chicago. They'd offered beds to Mobe and wound up with the *Newsreel* crew. The wife served us slices of melon and explained that it was a very rare and special kind that they had picked up on a drive to California. She cooked us bacon and eggs and made a big pot of coffee. The meal made me feel like a guest in a home instead of a vagabond camping out. When her husband was out of the room, the wife told us he wasn't all that interested in educational psychology, but, of course, graduate school was a good way to beat the draft.

We watched the news on television. The Attorney General had ordered an investigation of Wednesday and the whole Chicago police force. Good news. Then Dave Dellinger came on. He announced that Mobe was going out of business. They were retiring to a farm outside Chicago to rest and discuss the events of the week.

Ken wanted to see what was going on at Lincoln Park and I wanted to find out what had happened to Keith so we went up together. We stopped first at Jay's apartment. It was almost noon and there was no sign that Keith had even been there. And the telephone was disconnected! I cautiously pulled back the curtain in the front room. The sun was shining brightly and the street looked quiet enough, but it was filled with cars. More cars it seemed to me than I had ever seen there before.

"It's a stakeout!" I yelled to Ken. "Let's get the hell out of here."

I gathered up my notes, everything that might be even the slightest bit incriminating, and ran to the post office. I felt better when they were safely in the mail, addressed to my wife. At least nothing I had written down could get anybody into trouble.

Coming back, I walked north along Wells Street. It looked as if the people from Lincoln Park had completely occupied the phoney bohemia of Old Town. They filled the restaurants and talked in little groups on corners or just sat on the curb, enjoying the sun. Everyone gave me the V sign. We were all veterans now. We were all brothers.

I found Ed Sanders at the Lincoln Hotel. He had heard from Keith, who was fine and coming back to Jay's, but Jerry Rubin was still being held on $25,000 bail. The cops were charging him with solicitation to commit mob action. A movement lawyer said that was still only a misdemeanour despite the ominous sound. However, that charge was probably only the beginning. The cops would probably make the charge a felony as soon as they could.

I called Jay again and found out what had happened to the telephone. Someone had called her late at night, collect, all the way from Alabama. The caller had asked for Doris, the girl who had crashed there Monday night. He told Jay that Doris had given him the telephone number and the address and told him he could stay there when he came to Chicago. Jay told him to go to hell and unplugged the phone. In the morning, she was still so mad at Keith and me that she had the telephone disconnected. But later, she had calmed down and now she was having the phone put back into working order.

I felt like a damned fool. Stakeout? Nonsense. Talking to Jay brought me back to the real world.

But I was still glad I had mailed out my notes. In the real world, the cops were still holding Rubin in jail and his friends were still trying frantically to raise bail for him. It was better not to have anything around that might get him into even more trouble.

There were only a few people in Lincoln Park. The Yippie show was over there. I went back to Jay's to rest a little and then took a bus down to Grant Park. I found Keith and Ed Sanders on the corner across from the Hilton. They were waiting for the last Yippie pig. Someone was supposed to be bringing it down by car and they were going to release it in the park.

Grant Park was still littered with paper. The people I

had become used to seeing in Lincoln Park wandered around like grey, red-eyed ghosts. Wolfe Lowenthal came by with a bandage on his forehead and a cast over his hand. A cop had caught him with a blackjack during the fight around the flagpole. A television reporter came up with some news of Rubin. Did we know that a motorcycle kid who had offered to be Jerry's bodyguard had turned out to be an undercover cop? In fact, it was the motorcycle kid who suddenly turned on Jerry and made the arrest. Keith became very agitated. As far as we knew, he wasn't being tailed, but the cops must certainly know all about him. "This long hair makes me a target," Keith said. "I feel they're going to pick us up now, one by one, in the street."

McCarthy had just finished speaking in the park but nobody seemed impressed. He'd said something about how he could see that he still had a constituency. Some constituency! There were only about 300 people still hanging around the park and they didn't look like the kind of people who would just slip back into the old politics again. Doris, the girl from Alabama, came up to say hello. She had left Mel, the Resistance fighter from New York, and had taken up with a much straighter-looking boy. He had a bright California suntan, sports clothes, and short, curly hair. But Doris still looked woolly-eyed. An elderly lady in a thin flowered dress marched up and down the sidewalk with a homemade sign. On a newspaper, she had written with black crayon, "Berlin 1938—Chicago 1968."

I found out that a gang of delegates had set out on their own little march to the Amphitheatre, so I set out to find them. I'd gone about ten blocks when I started meeting people going the other way. The cops had let them go for some distance and then suddenly swooped down on them at a tunnel under some railway tracks and blocked the march. Everybody was coming back. I returned to the park, too.

A huge crowd had gathered around the statue of General Logan. The statue was on a high grassy mound and this was now filled with people, all sitting quietly and waiting. Some kids had climbed right up on the statue and were sitting on General Logan's green bronze horse with an NLF flag. But they soon changed this for a black anarchist flag.

A line of cops formed in the street. A cop on a bullhorn warned us to stay in the park. We had a right to hold meetings in the park. We would be protected in the park. But we had no permit to hold a parade. If we attempted to march again, we would be subject to arrest.

But at the same time, someone with a bullhorn in front of the statue was telling us that we definitely were going to march again. And this time, not the cops, not the army, not anyone was going to stop us. We were going to the Amphitheatre. Hurray! Hurray!

This was my most frightened moment. Before, there had always been Mobe or the Yippies or somebody organizing the show. But Mobe had left town and the few Yippies who had played leadership roles were spent or wrapped in bandages or in jail. This march looked like it was going to be a mob action, small bands of people running in all directions, trying to make it in any way possible to the Amphitheatre. And the cops would be able to whip along in the squad cars picking everybody off. There would be no television cameras this time and nobody would see or know what was going on. I hated the people egging the crowd on through that bullhorn because I knew I was going to have to go along with whatever they did. I no longer had any control over what was going to happen to me. I had become part of the movement. Listen to the bullhorn. Follow the leader.

But Dick Gregory came, bless him. Gregory took over

the bullhorn and told us the cops were forbidding us to walk in the streets but we had a constitutional right to be in the streets. So he was inviting us all to exercise our constitutional rights and come on over to his house, which just happened to be in the direction of the Amphitheatre. Now when we reached the corner of Michigan and 55th Street, we could turn off to his house or we could keep marching on toward the Amphitheatre. We would have to decide about that when we got to the corner. But he was just inviting all of us over to his house. He was exercising his constitutional right to invite his friends to walk in the streets with him.

The National Guard came and lined up on the road replacing the cops.

But I still felt better. At least we were going to be on a march. We would be an organized body of citizens, not bands of guerrillas running through the night streets. I went to the drinking fountain to wet my handkerchief and tie it around my neck for the tear gas.

Gregory introduced Pierre Salinger, who had come over from the Hilton to say a few words to the people. Salinger said he appreciated what we were doing and he wanted us all to know that while we were fighting the good fight out in the streets, there were other people inside the convention hall fighting, too. We all have to fight in our own way, Salinger said, and he was going to keep on fighting inside the established political context.

The crowd booed so loudly Salinger had to give up.

I saw Stew Albert and a couple of people from Rubin's band and I asked them if the story about the biker turning out to be an undercover cop was true. "Definitely not," Albert said. "That's the kind of story the cops start to drive us apart. Don't spread that story around."

The march took a long time to get going. We spread out

on the sidewalk in lines of three and we had to wait until Gregory got everybody organized and then ran to the front of the march with his bullhorn. I joined a line with Marj, the girl from *Newsreel*. She had got separated from the rest of her crew and wanted to go on the march. The third person in our line was a very young boy from Chicago. I don't remember his name, but we all shook hands and it was understood that the three of us would try to stick together.

It seemed as though we were standing on the sidewalk in front of the park for a good half-hour before we began to move. Delegates were scattered through the crowd. One of them in the row just ahead of us passed around pieces of pecan brittle from a brown paper bag. He said he was from Beverly Hills. He was a tall, wind-burned man who looked like he had once played bit parts in Western movies.

Behind us, a volunteer medic got on the bullhorn and announced that the cops had given notice that they believed the medics were directing all the demonstrators. This was why they were attacking the medics so viciously. He warned the medics to take off their white coats and Red Cross armbands.

The National Guard faced us with their rifles and some people called them pigs. But they were just kids and some of them surreptitiously gave us the V sign. We talked openly in front of the soldiers and someone pointed out that getting into the National Guard was one good way of staying out of Vietnam, so, in a sense, the Guardsmen were probably on our side.

The march moved out slowly, three abreast, punctiliously stopping at traffic lights. The National Guard stayed in front of the park. We were walking down the street and, except for a few squad cars, nobody was bothering with us.

We began to tell each other, hey, it's working. We're actually getting away with it. Maybe all the bad publicity from the beatings last night has got to the cops. Maybe they're just going to let us through. Fantastic! After all that fear and bloodshed, this time we're just walking to the Amphitheatre. We sang "The Battle Hymn of the Republic" and "America the Beautiful."

We were passing through a neighbourhood of factories, high, grey apartment houses and ragged vacant lots. Negroes stood in doorways and leaned out of windows. "Join us! Join us!" the crowd chanted. Some of them gave us the V sign, but no-one actually fell in with the march. A voice came at us suddenly over a loudspeaker, "Go on, get outa here! We don't need no hippies in Chicago! Go on back where you came from!"

We spotted the loudspeaker sitting in the fourth-floor window of a grimy old hotel across the street. Some people shouted, "Fuck you!" and so on, but most of us just laughed and kept on walking. There was such a sweet feeling of triumph. The sky was getting dark and the air was cool and smoky. The boy from Chicago said the test would come at 18th Street. We were already into the fringes of the ghetto, and once past 18th Street, we would be in the territory of the Blackstone Rangers. The cops had been afraid all week to let any marches into the ghetto for fear that Negroes would join them and start rioting. But a Negro girl behind us, a fat girl with gold-rimmed glasses who looked like a college student, said the Rangers were coming up to join us and the cops would let us go through because the cops didn't want to cross the Rangers.

On transistor radios, we heard the tumult in the Amphitheatre. The memorial film for Bobby Kennedy had just been shown and the delegates wouldn't stop cheering and singing. Daley and the convention chairman, Carl

Albert, were trying to shut them up, but the delegates were defying them. The spirit of Grant Park seemed to have reached out to the Amphitheatre. Who could tell? Perhaps the delegates would even march out and meet us halfway.

Truckloads of Guardsmen began to go by, and then the march slowed down and finally halted. Cars were being stopped, too. We chanted, "Stop here for peace! Park for peace!" trying to get people to abandon their cars and block the street, but most of them just turned around and drove back. Bob, Marj's boyfriend, caught up with our line. He had been looking all over for her.

The word went down the line that all delegates were needed at the front. Our pecan-brittle man from Beverly Hills left. We were standing and sitting on the sidewalk for half an hour before Dick Gregory came by with the bullhorn and told us that the cops and the National Guard had stopped us at 18th Street and he was negotiating with them to let us continue on with our walk to his house. But the cops had said that anybody who went past 18th Street would be arrested. If any of us didn't want to be arrested, we should leave now. Nobody left.

We began to discuss getting arrested. There looked to be about 3,000 people strung out on the sidewalk behind us. Where would they put us all? Someone suggested Soldiers' Field. There was also a report that the army had concentration camps already set up outside Chicago and they would take us out to them in trucks. Groovy! That would really expose the American military machine. But would they feed us? It was already eight o'clock at night and maybe they wouldn't feel obligated to give us any food. Except for breakfast with the young couple and a little pecan brittle, I had had nothing to eat all day.

Word went down the line that Dick Gregory and the

delegates had been arrested. We pressed forward and I could see the intersection then. It was illuminated with bright searchlights. The National Guard had formed up across the roadway and it was like they had completely packed the street beyond it. They were grouped around an armoured personnel carrier that had a machine gun mounted on it. I saw Art Goldberg of the *Ramparts Daily Wallpaper* and asked him if he was carrying his press credentials. He said he didn't have any. "I'm a demonstrator first and a reporter second."

A Negro in a brown denim jumpsuit came back to the crowd with a bullhorn. He said that we were now going to march through the intersection, and as soon as we crossed 18th Street, we would be arrested. We should form threes, link arms and start marching. We put Marj between us, and Bob and I took the outside tracks. We linked arms and began to move up. But we got only a few feet before we were up against a solid wall of people. And the crowds behind us were still pressing in.

We were tightly packed when the tear gas started. One of the first canisters landed a couple of feet away from me. It was made of khaki cardboard and was about the size and shape of a tin of baby food. It spun around on the road, spewing out white plumes of gas.

The tightly packed crowd evaporated. Bob pointed to a vacant lot between two buildings. We started down it. The street behind us was filling up with gas. People were running and screaming and trying to hold wet handkerchiefs over their faces. I had mine tied around my neck and I pulled it over my mouth and nose, but it didn't do much good. The gas filled my eyes and seared my throat. A crowd followed us into the vacant lot. But then people ahead of us were running back, colliding with us. Gas filled the narrow space between two buildings. And through the white cloud, we could see the cops in gas masks advancing slowly at us. A trap! The cops had sucked us into a trap! I lost Marj and Bob. Beside me, a boy suddenly spun around and fell and began sobbing hysterically. People bent over to help him and I joined in. It took six of us to subdue the kid and carry him out. The cops were almost on us. We had to hoist the kid to our shoulders and run with him. His feet were still kicking out wildly and he was moaning and screaming.

The street was filled with gas, but the cops had not yet begun to advance through it. We were able to get out to the street and find a medical team. The kid had calmed down a little and the medics had us carry him into a gas station, where they had water. I dipped my own handkerchief into the bucket and daubed my eyes. The temptation to rub them was almost irresistible.

I went back out to the street and found Marj and Bob. Marj had been hit by something but she wasn't sure whether it was a rock or a police club. Anyway, she wasn't bleeding. The medic gave her some water for her eyes and sent her on her way.

The cops were firing tear gas ahead of them and slowly advancing through it. Some people fought back with stones and pieces of brick. We came through one cloud of gas and there, like an apparition, was a ring of National Guardsmen. They must have moved in behind us. They had their gas masks on and their bayonets pointing out and they were guarding a jeep with a Goddamned machine gun on it.

"Walk, walk, walk," the chant went up and we walked. There were no leaders now but the game was obvious. Make the cops chase us all the way back to the Hilton. Make them fire their tear gas into the crowds of straight people. We formed lines, linked arms, waited until the gas came and then fell back. The street was getting wider now and the gas dispersed quickly. Marj was still feeling shook up from whatever had hit her in the vacant lot and Bob slipped down a side street with her and took her home. We had lost the boy from Chicago and I was all alone now, but I didn't care. I felt ready to be on my own and look after myself.

We were moving now into the bright lights section of Michigan Avenue again. We could see the Hilton. There were cars now, too, trying to honk their way through the mob. We warned them to roll up their windows. The cops were almost on us again with tear gas. One man handed out Kleenex tissues and then drove off.

I met the schoolteacher from Maryland whom I'd been running through the streets of Old Town with on Monday night. He said he'd been clubbed that night after we got separated, but it hadn't been too serious and he was all right now. He was still wearing his old army shirt. And he had a friend now, a young, tough-looking Negro, and it was clear that they had formed their own little affinity group. A gas canister landed beside us and the Negro boy grabbed the schoolteacher's arm and pulled him away.

The Guard had formed a large semicircle guarding the Hilton and we began to pour into the park again. A kid started running at the soldiers, screaming, "Pigs! Fucking pigs!" at them. I put my arm around his shoulders and gently led him off. "Easy, brother, easy. Our time will come."

Hell, I was even becoming a leader.

People who had got to the park ahead of us had started fires in the trash baskets. The crowd was screaming. We gathered around the bullhorn, our link with the outside world. An effigy that was supposed to be Mayor Daley but just looked like a fat scarecrow was hanging from a tree and burning brightly at the front of the park.

Tear gas again. Fired into the park for the first time. No more sanctuary there. The National Guard advanced slowly, rifles pointing out, into the park. We ran. It looked like this was going to be the final, bloody climax to it all. They were going to clean out the park in front of the Hilton. I got into the section of park one block north and then turned back to see what was happening.

The Guard was pulling back. They pulled down the effigy and stamped out the flames and put out all the fires in the trash baskets and then withdrew to their line on the roadway.

I found one of the kids we had had supper with the night before. He was travelling barefoot. The kid was alone, too, so we sat down together on the curb to smoke a cigarette and discuss what we should do next. The Guardsmen had re-formed their semicircle in front of the Hilton and the cops were beginning to spread out around us. We decided to rejoin the crowd in the park. I was afraid we would get cut off from the main group of people.

But the park scene was cooling out. The bullhorn was telling people to sit down and they were beginning to relax on the grass. They were even beginning to sing folk-songs. It was turning into a rally. We decided to get something to eat and we went back to the all-night pizzeria on Wabash Avenue. It was almost midnight, and I called Keith to tell him what had happened. He said that the pig had never showed up and he and Ed Sanders had left the park early.

We were dead tired, but the barefoot kid and I decided to take one last look at the park. We found Super Joel and sat down with him for a while. Super Joel said he had been arrested three times but he wasn't planning to stick around for any trials. He and his band of anarchists, the Buckingham Affinity Group, were planning to move on to New

York. They had come to Chicago from Berkeley. Joel said he was married and had a four-month-old son. His wife had a three-year-old child by a previous marriage. The Buckingham Affinity Group was staying with his sister in a suburb of Chicago. His father was a big shot in the Mafia and some of the cops who arrested him treated him like an old friend. They remembered him from all the time they had spent tailing his old man. But he and his father hadn't spoken to each other for years. Super Joel said he was only nineteen years old. He believed in the psychedelic revolution. "You've got to tell the truth when you're on acid. You can't lie on acid. Acid makes you tell the truth."

Super Joel said he had started as a pacifist. He had been a member of the Port Chicago project, and for two years he had demonstrated non-violently in Port Chicago, California, against the shipment of war materials to Vietnam. The demonstrators had been frequently attacked and beaten. But Super Joel had stayed non-violent until the Pentagon march. There he was photographed sticking a flower into the barrel of a soldier's gun. The picture became famous but the Pentagon demonstration ended Super Joel's non-violence. Now he was an anarchist, plotting "psychedelic terror in the streets."

The park had become so peaceful that people were singing "We Shall Overcome." Super Joel sang, "We shall overthrow, we shall overthrow, we shall overthrow some day.... Oh deep in my heart, I do believe, we shall overthrow some day." A straight, portly, middle-aged man was sitting beside Joel. He slapped him on the leg and said, "You're all right, kid. You're all right."

It was two in the morning and I figured that nothing much more was going to happen in the park and I went home. The barefoot boy and some friend of his felt the same way and they came, too. I fell asleep in the cab. I woke up suddenly and we were driving into Lincoln Park and the tear gas was coming at us again through the trees. But it was just a nightmare. We were turning into Willow Street. I climbed the stairs to Jay's apartment. I was going to call the *Star* to see if they wanted a story from me that night, but I made the mistake of sitting down to rest for a minute on the couch, and I fell asleep.

New York, 1968

3

"Dirk, it may well be that I don't understand the meaning of romance," I say. "But I remember once I was going down the street — things always happen to me when I'm just going down the street because I'm a pisces and I attract energy like a lodestone — and this girl, she had a way of walking, free and easy like, with her hair blowing in the wind and her sandals not even touching the sidewalk, like those dirty old streets were really just fields of flowers, and I said, 'Come home with me now. I will love you forever as soon as you tell me your name.'

"And she cried, 'Oh yes, I'm coming!' And I came too, and we lay together on a lumpy mattress and I thought, 'Oh Jeez, isn't that something now. We must be supercompatible because we make the big pink cloud together the first time, dead on together.' Afterwards she washed out her little red net bikini panties and hung them over the electric heater to dry. I went out and panhandled enough to buy some wheat germ and celery stalks and after supper we did it again, rolling toward each other like wild young gazelles. This time the walls of the room dissolved and enveloped us and we went soaring hi-ho over the great

Ohio and I thought we'd never come down again.

"When her panties were dry, we went to the demonstration. I gave her my old helmet liner and my bayonet and these probably saved her life. We were marching on the Indian embassy to protest the raising of the dhoti in Madras State. We, of course, were anti-dhoti and pro-free-trade. We wanted to show our solidarity with oppressed dhoti growers of Madras and all the victims of neo-colonialism throughout the third world.

"We wanted cops to attack us because the movement needed street fighters, hungry revolutionaries gnawing from within at the soft underbelly of the great beast, imperialism. And the only way to produce street fighters was by street fighting. Like the song says, you've got to be taught to hate.

"So we marched up from Boysenberry Square to embassy row near BigTown Heights and the cops attacked us just as we rounded the corner of the National Brewery Building. They had been waiting all day there for us and we heard later that the National Brewers had been giving them free refreshments. The cops were all revved up and raring to go by the time we got there.

"They came crashing through our lines with their squirts of mace and steel-tipped lathis and God, I was so proud of her. Two cops fell on her and she bit one in the leg and got the other square in the belly with the bayonet. All the way up to the hilt she hit him. She came up for air with his blood running down her blonde hair and bleached blue jeans and she cried out over the din, 'Peace now! Peace now! Peace now!'

"I tried to get to her but I got hit from behind and woke up in the old Number 5 police station. Seventeen other people had been arrested at the demo and they took us all down to night court and charged us with disorderly conduct. It was seven and a half hours before I was out on the street again and I ran all the way back to my pad. But I knew even as I chugged breathlessly up the stairs that I might just as well have walked.

"My Fugs record was still warm and there was a note on the arm of my stereo saying she had tried to say goodbye but she couldn't wait any longer for me because life was out there waiting and she had to keep moving along.

"I never saw her again. But whenever I come across a Madras dhoti or a pair of red bikini panties, I think of her and the tears come again."

Toronto, 1970

Fresh Disasters

I have had enough of dying. All the best people are going. A whole generation is sinking into the earth. I have stood now at too many gravesides. Sometimes I have wept and sometimes I have looked down at my shoes and wondered why I could not cry. But always I have been there; I have done my duty. Now I want an end to it. I want a truce, a lull. I need time for the bleeding inside to stop. I will sit here quietly sipping martinis until it no longer seems so terribly important that we buried Alec Reisman this afternoon. If I am very still, if I disturb no-one, make no demands, perhaps the gods will be kind. I will not start thinking about my wife's face. Susan was standing in her place of honour before Alec's open grave. I looked at her expecting the usual cold detachment, or better still, a healthy sneer, something to help get us both through the day. But when she turned to me, Susan's face was gaunt, grey, worn down like a piece of driftwood. She looked at me with pity in her eyes.

In the past year I have lost my mother, my grandfather, and two uncles. Then I have been surrogate, a dutiful agent from the past, at funerals for three of my father's friends. Now Alec. There is no-one left of my parents' generation. In my family, I am now the eldest male child, and if there were any family left worth speaking of, I could claim to be the head of it. But my sisters are scattered from Montreal to San Diego, and I have not seen my cousins in years. We are, as I tell my students in Sociology 127, split at last into nuclear units.

The peasants have made their final break with Europe. It has taken three whole generations and God only knows how much labour and thwarted love but now, a triumph of sorts—a little triumphant music, please, as we fan out to our townhouses and suburban estates—now we are independent and free. No more loyalty demanded to those grotesquely extended families, those smelly ranks of uncles and aunties our history obligated us to love, honour and, if necessary, support all the rest of our days. It has taken three whole generations to heal the trauma of separation from the Old World but now, at last, we are free. A few dances of liberation please, romantic *pas de deux* and tap-dance solos. The only people who can command our love now, as a legal and moral right, are our spouses and our 2.3 children. Or, as in my case, since Susan and I are waiting only for the final decree of our divorce, we are responsible only to ourselves.

This is not what my grandfather came to this country seeking. It's not what my father struggled all his life to achieve. I'm not even sure it's what I really want. One does not always choose to be part of great historical movements. But I do have it and I am trying to make the best of it.

I have begun to live in historical time. All the people I know and care about, I have known for at least twenty years. How much have I changed in twenty years? How much did the world change between 1900 and 1920? Or between 1930 and 1950? How much have I changed since I first brought Susan to the roof of the Park Plaza Hotel and grandly told her this was my local pub? Outside, there have been wars and revolutions and liberations and oil embargoes and voyages into space. But in here Harold and Ray, the waiters who have always been here, came gradually to distinguish our faces among the happy-hour crowd and to stop by our table to say hello.

We were still graduate students then and it was terribly important to be recognized by ordinary people outside our tight little campus world. Acceptance by Harold and Ray was proof we had not yet become ivory-tower academics. After we got married, Susan and I liked to sit alone at the corner table in the early evening and watch the golden lights of the skyscrapers come on, a floor at a time. We liked to look out at the thickets of hammerhead cranes hoisting up still newer, higher slabs and towers. I suppose we identified with their assertion of power. We were coming of age, expanding very fast, and a new city was growing up to receive us. We never dreamed it would turn into a cold, taut city. Just as we never dreamed we could grow bitter as well as old.

When the kids started coming, Susan was too tired to sit in bars anymore. She was too tired for anything, if it came to that. But sometimes, maybe once every six months, we'd make it back up here after a movie. We'd find the place almost empty, even on Saturday nights. The smart people had moved on. Those hammerhead cranes had put up too many big new hotels with smart, new bars on their ground floors. The people who mattered were spread too thin; the community unravelled. Not even a trained sociologist like me can keep track now of where and when the interesting people pitch camp.

When Susan and I did come up here, we'd make for our corner table and order martinis like the old days and talk about the film we'd just seen. Then I'd recognize the signs. Susan's eyes would begin to close and her head would nod. It was a toss-up whether she could finish the drink before her eyes closed and she began to drool and snore. Harold always walked with us out to the elevator and told us we should come up more often.

Well, he must be pleased now. The roof bar has been remodelled, tarted up really, but at least one of the old gang doesn't seem to mind. I've become a regular again. Harold and Ray are very discreet. When I come with a date —I still can't get used to the idea, a man my age going out on dates—they give me the big hello and show us to our table and ask how things are going. Then, after I've introduced my date to them, they quietly slip off so we can chat with uninhibited intimacy. My dates are always impressed. I am still in what my friends tell me is the Lolita / Pygmalion stage of being single. Later on, they say, when I have proven myself, I will be ready for mature women again. I certainly hope so. I'm bored already. Only when I am alone does Harold stop by as in the old days for a good long chat about handball and people and the state of the world. All this has taken twenty years of historical time.

I despise talking so much about Susan and my personal life. Broken marriages abound. They have become a cottage industry. Every person is unique, of course. How I love it when my students solemnly inform me that every single person in the world possesses his own special, unduplicable combination of qualities. There's nothing like a touch of education to over-extend the adolescent ego. Ah, yes, I tell them. It's true that every person is unique but every divorce is exactly the same, just like every happy family. So how do you fit that into your conceptual framework, eh? No matter whether they begin with violence or sweet reason over candles and wine, they all end in bitterness. It does not matter whether the parties begin by hating each other, they will surely hate each other by the time it is all over. They announce with a giant sigh of relief that at last they are free and, poor dears, they will never be free again.

I really should go home. But I am afraid someone will telephone me with news of some fresh disaster. Have I heard whose marriage has just broken up? In my circle of friends I count five marriages, including my own, that have gone down the drain this year alone. And do I know that so and so has gone psychotic? Yes, he tried to kill the *au pair* girl with nail scissors and his mother had him committed to the Clarke. And somebody has just lost his job and such and such a firm of hot-shot young lawyers is coming apart like a shattered glass, and somebody else has just been denied tenure at the university. His wife's pregnant and what's the poor bugger supposed to do? Teach public school? And someone else has died. The funeral is tomorrow, ten o'clock at Benjamin's. Shiva at the daughter-in-law's. In lieu of flowers please send contributions to the cancer fund. This has been a very bad year, and I can't take too much more of it. I have become very thin ice and the pressure of a child's sob could shatter me.

The trouble is, if I stay here much longer, I will become a fresh disaster myself. It does not matter that I have known Harold and Ray for twenty years of historical time —if I become embarrassing, they will throw me out. And if I make a public fool of myself, how can I come back here? There are so few places now where I feel safe.

Still, this is a risk I will have to take. I do not want to close my eyes until I have drunk so many martinis I can see only the cozy black insides of my own eyelids. I do not want to close my eyes and hear again Alec Reisman's dry, sardonic voice like slippers trampling over eggshells.

"Everything we produce gets turned into capital. In a capitalist society, we are all businessmen. Look at the poet! What does he do after all? He takes his nice feelings, he packages them with a pretty title, and he sells them in the marketplace. You think you're a big-shot university professor. But, personally, I see no difference between us. You package your brains and the university puts them on the shelf like you were a box of corn flakes. The university peddles you just the way I sell condominium apartments."

"The difference is, I am still trying to improve my life, to become a self-conscious human being. And you've given up. You sold out years ago. Yeah, you're so rich now, so cultured, eh? You can quote Karl Marx chapter and verse. But in your soul you're still a little peasant boy from Europe, mean and bloody-minded."

"Did I ever deny it? This country is no different from Europe. The only difference is, in Canada the peasants have all the money."

Alec Reisman was my father's best friend. A few facts. They grew up together, sold newspapers together, played basketball together, went to high school together, and, I think, even lusted after the same women together. I suspect my mother must have been one of them, although God knows why she chose my father. But something traumatic happened very early on in all their lives. Close as my father and Alec were, Alec was never welcome in our house. I never remember our two families sitting down to supper together. It was always my father going out to play golf with Alec or Alec coming over very late at night, after my mother had already gone to bed, to kill a bottle of whisky and argue with my father. I would lie in bed listening to them shout at each other and bawl each other out, and I would wonder how they could still say they were friends.

They joined the Young Communist League together. Looking back, my father used to say he was young and foolish but it was the Depression and the world was going to hell and only the Communists seemed to have any idea how to save it. And he was a Jew and the only leader in the world standing up to Hitler then was Stalin. Besides, he used to say with a chuckle, the Communists gave the best parties. If my mother was close by, he would pat her bottom and she would blush and wriggle away. It was the only sign of affection he ever allowed himself to show her in public.

Alec was more like what the Communists had in mind. He liked to tell people that when he was growing up, "There were the poor people, and then there was the Reisman family. We were the lowest of the low." My father used to tell a story to illustrate what Alec meant. One summer they were both supposed to be going off to a camp for two weeks. Some church was getting kids off the street because of the polio epidemics that used to hit the city every year. So Alec and my father signed up and the morning they were to go to the country they came with their mothers to the church steps. Everybody got on the buses and they began to pull away—all except the last bus, with Alec and my father inside. They wondered what was going on. Finally the door opened and the bus driver got out. When he came back, he called out Alec's name. Alec had to get off and my father and the bus went away to summer camp without him.

It turned out that even though this was a charity camp, the kids were supposed to bring two dollars. This was to cover the cost of chartering the bus. Neither Alec nor my father had explained this to their parents. They were about eight years old at the time. My grandmother always had a few bills in her little black coinpurse. But in Alec's family, two extra dollars was unheard of. His father was a plasterer but he had a crooked spine and seldom was able to work a full week. In her whole life, I'll bet Alec's mother never had two dollars to spare. And apparently, there was nobody around that day, neither from the camp, nor the bus company, nor the church, who would let her off the hook. So they kicked Alec off the bus and he never did get to go to a summer camp.

"My mother cried all the way home," Alec told me. "It didn't bother me so much. I was an active kid; I could always find things to do in the street. But the humiliation for my mother, that was something I never got over."

My father and Alec didn't last long as Communists. The Hitler-Stalin Pact finished off my father. If Stalin could join with his worst enemy, then how could anyone ever trust the Communists again? What was going to happen to the Jews in Europe? What was my father to say to the Norman Bethune Club he organized among the medical students? My father stomped out of the party, bellowing curses at Stalin and Tim Buck. Alec, however, simply shrugged off the Pact. If Tim Buck said the alliance was nothing more than a shrewd tactical manoeuvre by Stalin, that was good enough for Alec. When Hitler attacked Poland and the party was outlawed in Canada because of the Pact, Alec went underground. He used to talk about that as though he had been in the wartime underground, but really, not much happened. Alec changed his job and shortened his name but he stayed at home, living with his mother. The cops never bothered him. I don't think they were very serious about catching the Communists and, anyway, Alec wasn't very important. When Hitler attacked Russia and Stalin was a hero again, Alec joined the Air Force. After the war, he never went back to the Communists, not for ideological reasons but because he was too busy. The war made all the difference to Alec.

When it started, he was just another kid from Spadina Avenue hanging around pool rooms and shooting craps in alleys. If it hadn't been for the Young Communist League he would probably have wound up a bookmaker or worse. Then the Air Force took him and made him a radar technician. Alec said the Air Force was the first time he realized he was smarter than most other people. After he got out, he used his credits to study accountancy and open his own office. Later, he went into partnership with one of his clients and they were spectacularly successful. Their Happy Times Development Co. built shopping centres and apartment buildings all across Canada and in Florida and Texas.

Yesterday, the newspapers told with such eloquence the story of how Alexander Charles Rice, the poor immigrant boy from Lithuania, had risen from his humble origins to become one of the wealthiest men in Canada. Nobody mentioned that Alec had once been a member of the Young Communist League. The editorial writers didn't even talk about the time Alec organized the famous three-day student strike at Long Road Technical School. Yet Alec always credited the Communists with teaching him how to be a successful businessman.

"The only philosopher who ever understood human nature was Karl Marx," Alec liked to say. He said it so often it sounded like a speech to a service club. "Marx taught us that everything that exists in the whole world is produced by human labour. And everything is for sale. There is only one question still to be decided: who is going to get all this wealth everybody is producing? The Communists used to say they should make that decision in the name of the working class. But one day I thought, 'Why them and not me? Why should the big shots in the party have all the fun?' So now I'm a capitalist and a miserable exploiter of the working class. But I'll tell you something: I give away more to charity every year than the Communists collect in dues from their whole membership. And I'll tell you something else: I do a thousand times more good with my money than they do."

Yet for all his talk about hard times and the Communists, the closest Alec ever got to a real revolutionary situation was when he came to visit me during the Columbia student strike. I was quite a shock to him; I enjoyed it thoroughly. My head was wrapped in bandages and blood caked my face. I told Alec the world was never going to be the same again. It sounds funny now, but it was real enough then. The Students for a Democratic Society had taken over five buildings and held them for a week. Finally the administration sent for the cops. The cops busted the students inside the buildings and then smashed everybody they found on campus, the left, the jocks, the liberals—even the campus rabbi got his head cracked. Next morning the cops were everywhere, like an occupying army. There were so many student factions Columbia felt like a civil war. Even Alec was impressed. When he found me, he held me at arm's length and then embraced me. He even kissed me.

What they only talked about, I did. The Communists waited for the revolution like hitch-hikers waiting for a ride. But I was there. I screamed, "Up against the wall, motherfucker" at the cops and I held my ground when they came at me with the blackjacks. I was lucky to get away with my life. I was there. I have eleven stitches in my head to show for it. I was part of a real uprising and nobody will ever be able to take that away from me.

Spring in New York that year, 1968, really did feel like the beginning of a revolution. Years of anti-war demonstrations had finally driven Johnson to announce he would not run again. Incredible as it may sound now, the president of the United States was afraid to show his face in the streets. Then an assassin shot Martin Luther King. Blacks rioted in ten American cities. The country was on fire. It hadn't come to New York yet, but everybody knew it would. Everybody was into some kind of politics. They went all the way from the sweet, ancient pacifists of the War Resisters League to the underground guerrillas who were already holding seminars on how to plant bombs. There was even something called "Dial-A-Demonstration." You could call up and find out how many things were going on that weekend. I used to go every Sunday to the big anti-war demonstrations in Central Park. I was doing research for my doctoral thesis; my subject was the kinship relations between members of the traditional left and the so-called New Left. My research showed that most of the new leaders were children of old-time Communists and party sympathizers. They inherited their radicalism just the way the Young Americans for Freedom inherited their conservatism. Newspapers used to say there were 50,000 or 75,000 demonstrators at those Central Park rallies but the newspapers lied. Newspapers always lie. We filled the whole Sheep Meadow. Sometimes it felt like half a million people. Most people stayed in those very tight little groups — the feeling of paranoia was very high in those days — but the overall feeling was still very communal. People smiled at each other and shared their joints. There was so much smoke in the air you could get stoned just sitting there. Everybody sang about love, and talked about love; some people even tried to look loving. Love was the only defence against the war. I wrote in my notebook, "The children of the middle class have been denied power so long they no longer want it. They insist on their right to remain children." That's a good one, eh? It's a pity I never finished my book about the New Left.

I was in Fayerweather Hall the night of the "Big Bust" at Columbia. I'd been going from building to building that night, taking notes on people's state of mind, when we got the word: the pigs were on campus. By the time they got to Fayerweather, the noise outside had grown to a roar of battle with sounds at the edge of breaking glass and people screaming. Through our high windows we could see television lights going on and off somewhere like a lighthouse beacon. And suddenly the police were there. They clubbed down the people on the steps of our building and pulled away our pitiful barricade of furniture and they were inside the building. For a moment, I remember, the roaring stopped. Everyone froze; there was absolute silence. We were all sitting on the floor and the cops facing us looked terrified, ready to kill us. Then somebody yelled,

"Up against the wall, motherfuckers!" and we all yelled it. It was a wonderful moment of defiance. I have felt ever since that I can face anything because I faced death that night in Fayerweather Hall.

I never even saw which cop hit me or what he hit me with. All I remember is somebody throwing me through an open door. I guess some cops on the other side were supposed to catch me and take me to a paddywagon. But no-one did. I just went on and on with my head bent over and streaming blood until finally I collapsed on the grass. Some medical students in white coats found me and got me off to a hospital.

I was lucky. No bones were broken. But it took eleven stitches to close the wound and they hurt like hell. I still get migraine headaches along the scar. In the morning, Alec found me and took me to his hotel. He was in New York raising money for his umpteenth apartment house. I was all set to quit school and join the guerrillas but Alec talked me into coming down to his hotel and resting for a few days. I suppose it was a good idea. I was in no condition to think clearly.

"I almost went to Spain," Alec told me over a bottle of Scotch in his room.

"What stopped you?"

"Who would look after my mother? My brothers were still babies."

"You should have gone," I told him. "You really should have gone." There was one thing I was sure I had got out of the Big Bust and that was a whole new understanding of education. I remember my notebook journal said that "Education is only the last moment before the cops come." In the liberated buildings at Columbia — or "occupied," depending on your age and orientation; I still think of them as "liberated" — everybody talked. Words became actions. The students themselves decided what had to be done and they did it instantly. But it wasn't only politics that occupied us: we listened to music; we talked about literature, psychology, films, everything under the sun. The tension was unbearable; everybody knew the cops would have to come. But at the same time, we were serene, our minds were open. We easily absorbed ideas it would have taken us years to assimilate in the boredom of a classroom. There was even a wedding in Fayerweather Hall when I was there. We stood in the stairwell holding candles and a minister with a dog collar performed a real ceremony. The couple were dressed in white and the bride had a little veil. The minister told them they were "children of the new age."

I wish I had kept the notes I made in Alec's hotel. I was working on a way to translate my great insight into practical teaching methods. I wanted to recreate the Columbia strike every time I entered a lecture hall. I was going to make every lecture I gave a confrontation. The job of being a teacher was to challenge students to the roots of their being.

I suppose that all sounds terribly pompous now. The truth is, I've become a very different kind of teacher and I don't have any theories of education any more. Pedagogical theories don't last long when you're facing students every day. Still, I don't think I was so wrong then. And I'm not ashamed of anything I did at Columbia.

In a way, I'm fortunate I never finished my book on the New Left. The scene changed so fast everything I had to say would have been outdated by the time the book came out. I know a lot of people who used to talk about "going into the street" and "picking up the gun." They get very angry now if you remind them of the things they said then. Some of them have even gone the other way; they've become full-time reactionaries. They seem to think the New Left collapsed just to confound their predictions and spite them personally. So they've turned reactionary to spite their old leaders. Or to spite themselves. I don't know. It's an idea I should work on some time.

The only long-term advantage of a book would have been to give me one more emotional card to play on Alec. I tried for years to make Alec respect me. I suppose I even wanted him to love me. But the only person Alec respected unconditionally all his life was my father. He used to tell me my father was a saint—even if he did get rich on other people's misery. But my father was not a saint; he was not even kind. And Alec must surely have known this. But even when I was a grown man myself and came to visit him with children of my own, Alec would never talk honestly to me about my father.

As I remember my father, he was always angry. The world was populated by fools, con men, thieves, pimps, bookies, rackos, hoods and on and on. Raging, that was my father; raging long into the night. The only acceptable people were his patients, and for them he would drive himself into a frenzy. On their behalf he fought with hospitals, insurance companies, landlords, even other doctors. A woman told me once how she came to him for a second opinion about an operation on her legs and he saved her life. Her own doctor wanted to tie off her veins and that would have left her a cripple for the rest of her life. My father examined her and decided the problem had something to do with her thyroid and he could cure her with medication. He called up her own doctor while she was still sitting in his office and bawled him out for giving such a sloppy diagnosis. Years later, the woman still recalled it all with amazement and delight. Right in front of her, my father called her doctor a pimp, a butcher, a money-grabbing whore, and every other name he could think of.

I suppose my father was loved by his patients. Or maybe they just respected him. Anyway, dozens of them came to his funeral, people I'd never seen before. But except for Alec, few people spent much time with my father. His outrage was too overwhelming. I always thought my father had the power to cast a black spell around him, making everybody he talked to angry at him or angry at the world. I've often pictured my father moving through life enveloped in a cloud of acid that burned anyone who got too close. The only place he felt completely happy was the operating room. There, nobody could talk back to him. My father loved the science of medicine and he was good at it. But he hated sick people. He hated weakness of any kind. Other doctors have told me how much they admired his skill but they were afraid to work with him. He'd rant and scream and bawl them out right in front of the nurses. Still, they all sent him patients and my father made a lot of money. Most of it he lost because he insisted on playing the stock market himself and he'd never listen to Alec's advice. But the other doctors told me there wasn't a surgeon in the city who worked as cleanly and as quickly as my father. There wasn't a surgeon in Toronto who did less damage to the patient than my father.

My father died at the age of 52. Perhaps, if he had lived longer, he would have mellowed and become a crusty but lovable old curmudgeon. But his life didn't work out that way. He was sitting with my mother one night after supper telling her what a useless bunch of whores the new surgery nurses were when he keeled over. His heart had stopped and he was dead within minutes. The firemen didn't even try to revive him. My mother was the only one there at the end. My sisters had all married and I was at Columbia. We had all cleared out of that rich, fearful house as quickly as we could. But my mother stayed on there alone for another twelve years. She finally died in January, diabetes and cancer of the bowel.

My father never paused long enough in his life to examine the roots of his anger. And I suppose there was really no reason for him to. He found the emotional energy generated by his sense of outrage a very useful tool in the practice of medicine. The closest I have been able to come myself to developing a consistent theory of his behaviour is to say that from the day he left the Communist Party to the day he died, my father was trying to prove that the Communists and Alec Reisman were wrong. My father insisted they acknowledge that there is such a thing as an unselfish man in the world. There are non-commercial, non-exploitative relations between people. "Look!" my father seemed to be saying, "I'm living it, aren't I? So what if other people are stupid, weak and greedy! Look at me! Am I not all the proof you need?" What ate my father up alive was the realization that neither the Communists nor his old friend Alec cared much what he did. They knew they were right. Dialectical materialism and human nature were on their side. I don't think anything my father could have done would have impressed them.

Alec gave me the money to finish my Ph.D. He paid off the mortgage on my mother's house and put me on the payroll of one of his companies. Then he took me out to lunch at his club and explained why he was doing it that way. He wanted me to have income free of my father's insurance so I wouldn't feel I was taking money from my mother in her time of need. And he wanted me on the payroll so he could claim the tax deduction on my "salary."

I collected that salary for five years. It carried me through the rest of my Ph.D. and a year of post-doctoral research in Vienna when I was supposed to be working on my book. I even used the money to get married on. I consoled myself by making silent promises to pay Alec back as soon as I was earning enough money of my own. I even approached him once with a first instalment. He said that hurt him more than anything else had in years. Accepting his money was the least I could do in memory of my father. And, anyway, it gave Alec such pleasure to see me get a good education. Who was I, Alec wanted to know, to deny him such a small enjoyment in his life?

"I have lived too long in your debt, Alec. You should not have expected me to be grateful. Surely the business world taught you that much. Nobody loves the landlord."

"You're still worried about the money? That's too bad; that kind of worry will keep you from growing up. I guess it's because you always worked for a salary, selling yourself off a little piece at a time. You're always afraid you'll run out of stock. It's only when you go out and actually make the money from other people—yes, like the Communists say, from the sweat of the workers—that you know what money is worth."

"It's not the money and you damned well know it. It's the idea. I know I have moved far beyond you. People can change within a single generation if they put their minds to it. I have left Europe far behind, I have risen far above the mean, frightened peasant class I sprang from. Yet you persist in your stubborn, irrational insistence that I am no better than you."

"If your life was such a big success, perhaps I would take

165

you more seriously. But look at yourself, sitting alone in a bar on the day you helped bury the last man in your father's generation who could have explained anything to you. *Regardez*! A paunchy romantic, slopping down martinis like a character in a bad love song. Look at yourself, middle-aged and getting fat, divorced and desperately needing the comfort and support of a woman, yet not knowing how to pay—there's that damned word again!— not knowing how to pay for that support by giving freely of yourself. Look at the mess of your life: an assistant professor of sociology who has just been granted tenure by the university and instead of celebrating, you're terrified."

That's true enough. I've been working all my adult life to gain a secure teaching position and now that I've got one, I'm more afraid than ever. Now that I'm a tenured member of the staff, the university will never fire me. I can stay there until I retire. But what if Alec is right, what if ideas are only commodities we buy and sell? And what if I have no more ideas to market? What will I teach for the rest of my life? What will my students think of me when I'm 50 years old? What will they say of me at 60?

Right now, I am still a good teacher. I wish I had been able to impress Alec with that before he died. When students are asked to evaluate their professors at the end of the year, they always give me the highest rating in the whole sociology department. I told Alec that a couple of times but he only smiled and said "That's nice." The only kind of success that counted with Alec—besides making a pile of money—was approval from above. Only if somebody rich or somebody powerful said you were good would Alec believe it. Alec died a fabulously wealthy man but he stayed a Communist and a peasant all his life. He never believed anything unless somebody in authority told it to him.

My relations with students were too intangible for Alec to appreciate. And anyway, these changed from year to year. Now that I am a tenured professor and I no longer need their approval, I am afraid that my attitude toward students is going to change permanently. I have lost my compulsive need to succeed with them. I am dreading what may happen in my classes this year. I am afraid I may already have begun to lose my nerve.

For a long time, I tried to treat my students as people. I listened to their troubles and I took them seriously even when they knew themselves they were not being very serious. Then it all came apart in my hands. And I don't know why. I didn't do anything foolish like start an affair with one of my students. But it did just hit me one day that I was enjoying all this a little too much. I saw suddenly that I was living vicariously off the energy of my students. It was what made me in their eyes a good teacher. But in my own eyes I suddenly saw myself as dishonest.

I was already into my late thirties. And there I was, spending all my time worrying about problems of twenty-year-olds. I was good for them because I had some experience of the world and I was a sympathetic listener. I could foresee consequences of decisions they had to make and I gave them useful advice.

The catch was, I had stopped dealing realistically with my own problems. I was so absorbed in, and so good at understanding, the troubles of the twenty-year-olds, that I got no pleasure at all out of coping with the demands life makes on a man who is getting down to the wire, almost 40 years old. I simply stopped handling my own life and instead became the very model of the always available, always sympathetic, altruistic university teacher. I think of it now as the Dracula syndrome. I had stopped living in my own historical time. I was poaching on my students' time.

I can hear Alec's broken, panting laughter as I say this. It was emphysema that finally killed him. But after 30 years of two packs a day, I suppose it was only a question of whether the emphysema turned his lungs to marble before the lung cancer turned them to ditchwater.

Alec would have said I was merely selling bits of myself to my students as well as to the university. Instead of letting the university package and market everything I had to offer, I kept back a little and went into business for myself. I was like one of those Russian peasants who produces three times as much on his own tiny plot as he does for a state-owned collective farm. There's a thought that would have amused Alec.

It would have amused my wife, too. She inherited Alec's sense of humour. We had a fair run at destroying each other, Susan and I. But as much as I have been — or probably ever will be—married to anyone, I was married to Alec Reisman's eldest daughter. I suppose that adds an extra dimension to my relationship with Alec—overtones, undertones, semi-tones, half tones. I don't know.

I don't think so. Susan and I managed to create quite a perfect little hell for ourselves without any encouragement from Alec. We didn't live with each other; we lived off each other. I don't think Alec ever fully understood how destructive we got. It was something we kept from him, a kind of tacit mutual agreement. That silence was the only honourable thing we did together in our six years of marriage.

No, the way I see it, Alec entered my relationship with his daughter directly in only two ways. The first was that Susan never knew the first two years of our marriage and the idyllic year we spent in Vienna were all paid for by my "salary" from Alec's company.

And the second is that Susan is living now with an architect and probably she is going to marry him. She knows very well that I consider architects the most hypocritical collection of prostitutes in our society. They talk all this jargon about "planes intersecting" and "tensions between spaces" and so on, trying to give people at dinner parties the impression they are so terribly concerned about aesthetics and "human values." Then they take commissions from ruthless little developers like Alec Reisman and put up cheap, horrible, ugly slab towers all over the city. The higher and more costly the building they put up, the bigger their commission. Alec always used to say architects were even easier to buy off than politicians. Architects were greedier. They'd cut any corner Alec told them to, as long as they got their money off the top. Then the architects go back to their cozy little associations and give each other prizes and gold medals for good design. As a social scientist, I find it highly significant that Alec's daughter should wind up marrying an architect. It shows that despite education and cultural conditioning, parental influence is still the dominant factor in her life. Susan Reisman is still a peasant.

I have coffee with her when I bring the kids back from my weekly outing. She tells me how happy she is. She says she is learning at last how to love another person. I have a hard time not to burst out laughing—as old Alec himself would have.

I wish Alec had lived longer. Or died earlier. As it is, he went at a particularly bad time. I had grown to depend on those lunches with him and those long talks into the afternoon. My own life is a little shaky right now. The future looks a little bleak. I have developed a great desire to explore the past. It is not just nostalgia. I despise nostalgia. But I would like to see my own roots more clearly. And feel them more. But now Alec Reisman is dead and my last connection with the past is broken. There is no-one left from my father's time to whom I can explain my life. There is no-one left to give me a blessing.

I think I should go home now. Tomorrow is visiting day with my kids and I don't want to go in feeling hungover and sick. Besides, it's closing time, right? Trying to get a drink after the last call is undignified. Harold and Ray would have to refuse me and I don't want to lose face with Harold and Ray. Not after all these years. I have a public face and I will not allow it to slip. That's something I learned from both Alec and my father. They practised it all their lives, a kind of old-school stoicism. Keep a tight grip on your emotions. Never let anyone know what you really feel, especially if they've managed to hurt you. Susan used to call it "cheap machismo" and I suppose she was right. She used to sneer at me for trying to be like Alec and my father. But once that kind of pride has been drummed into you, it's not so easy to give it up. I sometimes think I have reached a state of communion with my appliances, a mystic bonding with my microwave oven, my colour TV, and my quadraphonic sound system. Like them, I am solid state. I have no moving parts. I produce incredible amounts of work and the world applauds. But nobody ever sees how I do it. I am opaque. Unfathomable. Yes. But underneath, yes, I know only too well, the dry rot has set in. It's beginning to spread too—but slowly. I still have time left, I think. The dance of death is very lethargic. That's an image that seems to occur to me quite often these days. The waltz of death takes place in slow motion. That's my final thought for tonight. It takes longer than one thinks to die.

I really must go. I want to have some energy left for my

kids tomorrow. Sometimes I wonder if I look as large to my son as my father and Alec Reisman once looked to me. I'd like to think so. But I suspect I'd be kidding myself if I believed it.

Arnprior, 1976

In There

Pieter Xor-lil
Acting Commander
Sector Three
13/6/3826

Lt. Henri Xor-lil
Goldenberg Space Academy
Lin-tsu-7

My Dear Henri,
    You can scarcely imagine what pleasure it gives me to

finally address you as "Lieutenant." Your father would have been so proud. I know you will forgive me for using an old uncle's prerogative in having you assigned to Sector Three. You would probably have preferred the excitement of combat, keeping down the rim worlds in Sector Eight. Or perhaps you wanted to go exploring with the mad scientists in Comet Command. But Sector Three is still the heart of the Service. This is where your poor father was lost in the struggle with Goldenberg and Lin-tsu. That struggle continues to this day. Your father would have wanted you to play your part in it.

I think you will feel better about this when you come here and take your first trip on an inter-galactic cruiser. You will see then why the superstitious ancients used to call the passageways, "black holes." There is nothing quite like arriving finally at the very heart of the galaxy and finding instead of a blaze of stars and planets, only the zone of darkness. I have made the trip thousands of times now and visited galaxies beyond number yet I am still overcome with awe and even fear every time I enter the zone.

And nothing you have studied in school will prepare you for the elongation effect that takes place at the energy conversion point of the Goldenberg equations. When you see your own body as thin as a particle beam and know that you are suspended between space and time, that you have in fact overcome for a brief, crazy moment all the logic of matter, then I know you will feel what I still feel after all these years. This is one of the great wonders of space.

Your father gave his life that we might know this wonder. Now that you are a full-fledged member of the Service and a man of 55, I feel I can tell you the whole story. I am sure you will understand, and forgive, my part in it. For over 200 years now I have lived with a burning remorse. It sometimes seems that every night for 200 years I have seen your father in my dreams, belted into his little skip ship, careening wildly through the zone of darkness in that last bitter pursuit of Goldenberg and Lin-tsu.

I loved your father, Henri. It was not just that we were of the same clan. In these days of mass cloning and huge genetic corporations, who can say any more what blood two men of the same clan share? No, what bound your father and me together as close as the ancient animals was our love for the beautiful logic of space. We lived by the spaceman's rational trinity — matter, time and mind. We fought, and finally your father gave his life, to stop the stupid and dangerous mysticism of Goldenberg and Lin-tsu.

What a cult they have become! Your father would be overcome by outrage if he could see his son graduating from a space academy named after Goldenberg in a star system named after Lin-tsu. When we knew them, they were just a couple of space bums. Had there not been such a terrible shortage of bridge crew for the old freighters, they would never have been allowed into space at all.

Now I am sure it is only a matter of time until some new collection of fools begins a new cult and starts worshipping Goldenberg and Lin-tsu. I can hear them now claiming miracle cures and "peace of mind" from prayers to those two old frauds. Who would have believed that of all the ancient diseases, religion would return to haunt us again? Perhaps it's best your father never saw such a living mockery of everything we believed.

I can tell you now frankly that your father and I were sent to this sector because we had not done very well at the old Armstrong Space Academy. We were practical-minded and we could not bear sitting for days on end in the learning cubes. Those who did well — I've often thought they had strong bottoms rather than strong minds — all wanted to get into Sector Twelve.

It may seem like ancient history but it's only a generation ago that the pilots of Sector Twelve were trying to reach galaxies by direct flight. Even with the adaptations of ion-drive that hurled them seven, eight and even nine Einsteins past the speed of light, it took the better part of a lifetime to reach even the closest galaxies. Few of the Sector Twelve boys ever made it home again and those who did were withered, babbling old men. I wonder what the hot shots of Sector Twelve would say if they knew it was us, the lowly convoy guards of Sector Three herding ore freighters around the inner planets, who finally discovered the key to inter-galactic travel.

It all seems so simple now, a conical universe oscillating from the energy conversion cycle the ancients used to call the "big bang." I sometimes pity the ancients, riddled as they were with fear and superstition. All they could see were the galaxies rushing away from each other and by all accounts, this optical illusion so terrified them they went off on a religious binge much like the one infecting the world today. Well, I suppose the old navigator's saying still holds true, "All time is the same time when you're in hyperdrive.'

The ancients never dreamed of the invisible web of energy conversion that connects the galaxies like holes drilled through the cone. They thought the "black holes" were only burned-out and collapsed stars. But, really, one musn't sneer too much at the ancients. After all, it wasn't until Goldenberg and Lin-tsu that we understood it ourselves. My only wish is that your father had received credit for the great discovery, and not those old bastards.

Believe nothing they taught you in school about Goldenberg. He was only a dirty, quarrelsome old man who never took off that awful black skullcap, even when he was eating. He claimed to be a descendant of the ancient Jews and swore he had grown up in one of the living museums of Old Earth. But freighter crews who travelled with him told me he had never been closer to Old Earth than Gamma Six and everything he knew about the ancient Jews he learned from the cheap entertainment cubes. When he was high, he used to scream out that he had come into space looking for "Adonee" or something like that. The freighter crews, quite rightly, thought him crazy.

Compared to Goldenberg, Lin-tsu appeared quite rational. But only until you got to know him. Lin-tsu claimed a pedigree as ancient as Goldenberg's but at least he had papers to back him up. Lin-tsu was, certifiably, one of the last 200 genetically pure Chinese in the whole galaxy. He told me once when we were belting down flasks of heroin together at the old Gallipolitan Bridge (there was a bar I wish you could have seen!) that his ancestors had been priests in ancient China, keepers of the sacred books of Marx, Mao and Chan-sifu.

He had no papers to prove that part of his story but if it was true, he was just as much entitled to a place in one of the living museums as Goldenberg was. But instead of staying where he belonged, keeping the ancient traditions alive and talking to tourists, he had become a navigator for Goldenberg. The two of them belted around the inner planets causing more bloody trouble than all the rest of the Freighter Corps put together.

They had developed the charming habit of stealing freighters. That sounds ridiculous but I assure you it is the plain truth. Your father and I were nearly killed a hundred times running down the two of them and hauling them off to Service tribunals.

We'd get a call that Goldenberg and Lin-tsu were supposed to be hauling a load of base matter from Zerodin One to someplace like the third planet of Hephtus and they were two weeks overdue. We always knew where to find them.

Instead of skirting around the zone of darkness like rational spacemen, they would have plunged right into it, hundreds of light years off their plotted course. Goldenberg was still working on his equations and he had figured out the space-time co-ordinates enough that by playing a bit with his hyperdrive, he could get a whole generation into the zone of darkness before the gravitational pull of the passageway began to crunch his zoranium shield plates. They would hang suspended for as long as they could, pushing each time farther and farther inward. And much as I hated them then, I can sympathize with them a little now. I too have known the eerie wonder of that moment when all the logic of the universe begins to shrivel up and the body begins to experience the first stages of elongation.

We know now that this is only the approach to the point of conversion from velocity into energy and on through a pulsar and into another galaxy as reconstituted matter. But just imagine Goldenberg and Lin-tsu on the bridge of one of those rickety old freighters drifting inward through that. It's no wonder they came back to it again as though it were a drug.

When we were chasing them we, of course, did not have the advantage of even Goldenberg's rudimentary calculations. We knew nothing about the oscillations of hyperdrive to achieve free float. We had only the fragile power of our little skip ships against the overwhelming gravitational pull of the passageway. We were being pulled back and forth, every which way, like particles in a richochet acceleration chamber.

The closer in we chased Goldenberg and Lin-tsu, the

hairier it got with the whole ship rattling and buckling and the zoranium shield beginning to peel back like slices of cheese. We'd be screaming over the communicon threatening Goldenberg and Lin-tsu with 500 years in jail if they didn't turn back. But those bastards would turn the communicon right off. To get their attention we had to begin firing particle blasts at them. Only when we were actually burning up their landing pods would they finally turn back.

Then it was hell for breakfast out of the zone with all pipes blasting to escape the collapsing gravity of the passageway. Many's the time your father and I limped back to port in walkabout suits because the plates of the ship had been torn right off and we were leaking atmosphere like a sieve.

The Service tried dozens of times to put Goldenberg and Lin-tsu in jail. But the Freighter Corps always intervened. The inner planet freighters were cast-off wrecks in those days and only madmen would blast out in them. Madmen, as you know, tend to be somewhat scarce in space. So Goldenberg and Lin-tsu always got off with a small fine.

One of the things I'm sure they didn't teach you in the Goldenberg Academy is that Lin-tsu was a terrible drunk. It wasn't just that he could belt back enough heroin for a whole freighter crew, he'd order shots of disbellium and some of the harder stuff from the rim worlds.

When he was in his cups, he'd turn mean and start carrying on about evolutionary destiny and his "dialectics." I believe it had something to do with his ancestors, the keepers of the sacred books of old China. I never understood any of his drunken ravings, but when Lin-tsu was off on one of his tirades, Goldenberg would erupt too. Goldenberg was usually one of your quiet madmen but Lin-tsu had a way of getting to him and he'd suddenly start screaming about God and Lin-tsu would pour a flask of heroin over him and scream back that heroin was the only god. Goldenberg would leap for Lin-tsu's throat and the whole Gallipolitan Bridge would blast off into a three-siren riot. Then your father and I would have to wade into the midst of it with the Service Peace Corps to start cracking heads and hauling drunks out to the hoosegow in the asteroid belts. Oh, Lin-tsu and Goldenberg were real charmers, let me tell you.

Yet for all the trouble they caused us, I confess even now that there was something compelling about them. Perhaps it was only the power of their obsessions that separated them so sharply from the other human wrecks in the Freighter Corps. I remember once when they had pushed their luck too far and the gravity of the passageway had crumpled the plates of the quark generator, Goldenberg tried to fix it himself and took a heavy dose of particle radiation. I went to see him in the hospital and found a Service guard at the door. The leaking particles had killed three members of the engine crew. Goldenberg and Lin-tsu were no longer colourful eccentrics. They had been charged with criminal disobedience of Service procedure and they were facing heavy jail sentences.

When I entered the room, Lin-tsu was sitting beside the bed, holding Goldenberg's hand. The first thing he said to me was, "Did you come to make sure Jack was dead?"

But I was tired of the game. It had become too serious. I told Lin-tsu I was sorry about what had happened.

"Don't worry about us," he said. "We'll get out of jail. And we'll keep on looking."

"Looking for what? What in the name of the Hell Planets are you people searching for?"

"Jack says he's looking for God."

"Goldenberg is crazy," I said. "But you're a good

navigator. You could work anywhere in the galaxy."

"I'm trying to prove Jack wrong."

"Then you're as crazy as he is."

"My ancestors predicted paradise," Lin-tsu said softly. "They foretold that when man had destroyed all class distinctions and mastered the processes of production and distribution, man's soul would change and he would be filled with peace and sweetness. But that hasn't happened, has it?"

Goldenberg stirred on the bed. His face was horribly mottled from the particle burns and really, it was a wonder he was still alive. He tried to speak but what came out was only a bubbling little croak. Lin-tsu cradled Goldenberg's head in his arms and held a flask of heroin to his lips.

I felt pity for them then, locked into that barren steel hospital room. They were deluded and dangerous and they had to be stopped before they destroyed a whole freighter with all the crew aboard. But I understood that the bond between them was as strong as the bond of love that held your father and me together.

"Stop. Please stop." I was pleading with them but I felt no shame. I wanted only an end of it. I was afraid of having those two on my conscience forever.

"It hasn't happened yet but who is to say it will never happen?" Lin-tsu went on. His voice had reached that high-pitched tone I dreaded, the sound of a true cultist. "Most people do not realize my ancestors believed in evolution. It is implied in everything they wrote in their sacred books. Atheists and scoffers like you say that human nature has not changed in a hundred thousand years. Oh, I know all the arguments, we have better technology but men's souls are no better now than they ever were. What you poor ignorant people do not understand is that you cannot know the stages of evolution until you see the end of it. Who can say now what is progress and what is only blind mutation leading nowhere? All our science has brought us here, to the heart of the galaxy. Somewhere in there, inside that mystery you people call the zone of darkness, is the end of human destiny. I know it and poor Jack knows it. We just call it by different names.

"Adonai," Goldenberg cried in that bitter rasping voice. The heroin was beginning to affect him and his eyes were mellow and far away. "Adonai Elohenu. Adonai, Echod."

He passed out and Lin-tsu tucked him into bed as tenderly as one of the legendary ancient mothers might have cared for a child.

"Get out!" Lin-tsu said. "Leave us alone."

I never saw them again. Goldenberg and Lin-tsu went to jail and your father and I went to war. Goldenberg and Lin-tsu received life sentences for causing the deaths of three freighter crewmen, but by the time that news reached your father and me, we didn't care very much any more. We were combat pilots helping to put down the seventh rim world rebellion and we didn't expect to live very long. We were in at the battle of K-Stantin and the siege of the C-73 system and your father won his Galactic Cross in the final attack on the Actarene stars. I am sure you have heard of that battle. The Service turned Actarene into the first man-made nova.

Your father could have commanded the whole of Sector Three when we returned to the inner planets. But he refused to exchange the bridge of a spaceship for a steel office. So I became the sector chief even though I was only a major and your father had already received his first colonel's stars. Had he stayed here, he would have become one of the greatest galactic pilots of all time.

He would be here now had it not been for Goldenberg and Lin-tsu. Their last voyage is history now and I am sure you know how Goldenberg had been working on his equations in prison and how, when he and Lin-tsu were paroled to fly freighters during the war emergency, he began to plunge again into the zone of darkness. According to the history cubes, your father was just one of the minor obstacles they had to overcome. The cubes say your father was the stuffy bureaucrat who tried to stop them and then pursued them in a skip ship. They finally squeezed through the passageway and his ship was crushed. That's the way history records what happened. But history is wrong.

I remember so vividly the last time your father called me on the emergency frequency. He was chasing Goldenberg and Lin-tsu and they were already more than twenty generations into the zone of darkness. His zoranium plates had burned away and the inner shell was beginning to rattle. He was already beginning to feel a sense of elongation and his first words to me were a cry of fear.

But something else was happening too. He had fed Goldenberg's first three jumps into his ship's computer and the computer had fed back something close to Goldenberg's own equations. His hyperdrive was still working and even though his ship's superstructure was beginning to rattle apart, he wanted to keep going. Every time Goldenberg and Lin-tsu popped up on his vid screen, he fired another round at them. He was sure he would get them next time.

The official inquiry reprimanded me for not ordering him back. I had broken the operation code of the Service, risking a ship beyond reasonable doubt and endangering Service personnel. I have paid heavily for that split-second decision. I have been acting sector commander for almost 200 years but they have never made my position permanent and they have never raised me above major. Yes, I have paid over and over again but I have never regretted the choice I made that bleak morning in the Command Bureau.

It was my own brother I was talking to on the emergency band. He was one of the greatest fighter pilots to come out of the rim war, and he was chasing our old enemies. I told him to blast the bastards to the hell planets.

All communication stopped then. They were already into the full effects of elongation and it was several days before there was any sound over the emergency band. I grew frantic with worry and moved a cot into the Communicon Bureau so I could be there when we made first contact.

The first voice we heard was Goldenberg's. They had made it through the point of energy conversion and they could see an enormous light ahead of them. Goldenberg was praying in that bizarre ancient language of his. Then Lin-tsu took over and he was at least a little scientific. He told us about passing through the point of energy conversion and described the altered chemistry of his body. But he was convinced he had entered another universe. From somewhere, maybe one of his ancestors' sacred books, he had picked up the idea of several universes strung together like the beads of a necklace. He was absolutely convinced he had reached the evolutionary destiny of his race.

I wish I could have seen their faces when they shot out of that pulsar and found themselves in the centre of the L-24 galaxy. They must have thought they'd arrived in some primitive's version of heaven. Then the first Necturan warship approached them. According to the later reports we got from the Necturans, they tried to hail the old freighter on all possible bands. I wouldn't be surprised if Goldenberg answered them with ancient Hebrew prayers. He probably thought he was talking to God. The Necturans blasted them out of the sky.

Fortunately for the Service, Goldenberg had left a set of equations in his room at the Gallipolitan Spaceport. At the inquiry into your father's disappearance, the equations were brought in as evidence and one of the boys from Science Corps realized their significance. He started working on them and only ten years later the first ship from Sector Three made it through a passageway into another galaxy.

That's the true story of how Goldenberg and Lin-tsu became heroes with thousands of history cubes, biography cubes and entertainment cubes devoted to their sacred memory. I get ill just thinking about it. If the cubes mention your father at all, he is the villain, the stupid war hero who tried to stop Goldenberg and Lin-tsu right on the edge of their great discovery. Some even say your father deserved to die.

Well, wouldn't they be surprised to know that your father is still alive?

Yes, Henri, your father is still alive.

I've spoken to him three times since that last trip.

I'm afraid you will think I have lost my mind, that grief over my brother and my bitterness at the veneration of Goldenberg and Lin-tsu has deranged me. I wouldn't blame you if you thought this. The first time your father talked to me, I thought it myself.

I was herding a convoy of freighters through the outer asteroid belt of Hephtus and I heard his voice, very clearly calling my name and telling me he was well and happy. Without thinking I started answering him. I asked him where he was and why he didn't come home. Then I realized with a flash of sick horror that the communicon was off.

Henri, the communicon was off.

Your father was still alive somewhere in there and he was reaching out to me across generations of light years with some kind of telepathy. No, it was more than telepathy. He surrounded me. He overpowered me. I felt I was floating through some silent irridescent space of impossible happiness and he was my companion. It was more powerful than the strongest heroin I have tasted. He talked to me about such strange things, the physical overdrive of love, the hierarchy of sounds and the philosophy of particles. I didn't understand any of it.

That first communication lasted only a few moments although it felt to me as though I had been with him for days. Needless to say, I never mentioned it to anyone. I have spoken to your father two more times since then. He told me he was advancing in knowledge and would soon be one of the starmakers. He spoke of dancing in space. Dancing, Henri! And the last time he spoke to me, he said he was waiting for me to join him. There was so much to tell me, he said. So much to teach me.

Your father is still alive, Henri. Somewhere in there he is waiting for us. And together we will find him. You and I together, Henri, we will make such discoveries as Goldenberg and Lin-tsu never dreamed of.

Think of it, Henri, two space bums, survivors of ancient cults, went looking for God and some lunatic idea of the destiny of man and discovered only the passageways to inter-galactic travel. The laws of the universe governed them in the end and they govern all matter. But your father, a true spaceman who lived only to discover those laws, remains trapped somewhere in there.

Sometimes when the old wounds become too painful and I have belted down too many flasks of heroin trying to get to sleep at night, I think it would be the final irony if your father found what Goldenberg and Lin-tsu were looking for. But in the mornings, when I face the clear harsh lights of the Command Bureau, I know this could never be true.

When we find your father, he will tell us what he has learned and we will see that his discoveries conform to the logic of the universe. I am sure that your father has already done the preliminary reasonings and he is only waiting for us to find him so he can bring his hypotheses to Science Corps for testing.

Henri, it is not only your father that waits for us somewhere in there. Success, fame and a place for our clan in the history cubes wait too.

I know that you young graduates from the space academies like a little holiday before reporting to your assignments. And, certainly, after your twelfth-year finals you deserve a little time to let the pressure valves loose.

But even knowing this, I urge you to come here as quickly as you can. We have so much work to do. Grab the next freighter to the Gallipolitan Space Port. Just tell the captain you are coming to join me and he will be happy to have you aboard.

Welcome to space, my nephew. Welcome to the Service.

Your loving uncle,
Pieter Xor-lil.

Toronto, 1975

05